**He held up his cup.
"To a great assistant, whose help
this week has been invaluable."**

"To your family, especially the elders," Marissa
replied, her tone more serious than Donovan's.
"Whose vision made this day, and this moment."

And just like that the moment shifted. Her words
produced an awareness of who they were and where
they were and what they both felt but continued to
deny. Donovan's eyes darkened as he drank in her
countenance, focusing on the lips that she licked
when nervous, like now. Her eyes searched his as
well, noted the fast beat of his heart evidenced by
the throb in his neck. She broke the stare and took
a nervous sip of wine. But Donovan wasn't willing,
or able, to let the moment go so quickly. He leaned
over, slowly, as if dealing with a skittish mare that
might bolt from sudden movement, and placed the
lightest of kisses on her forehead.

"That was beautiful," he said, his eyes traveling
once more to her lips before moving back to her.

The moment was gone, but for both of them…the
memory lingered.

Books by Zuri Day

Harlequin Kimani Romance

Diamond Dreams
Champagne Kisses

ZURI DAY

snuck her first Harlequin romance novel at the age of twelve from her older sister's off-limits collection and was hooked from page one. Knights in shining armor and happily-ever-afters filled her teen years and spurred a life-long love of reading. That she now creates these stories as a full-time author is a dream come true! Splitting her time between the stunning Caribbean islands and Southern California, she's always busy writing her next novel. Zuri makes time to connect with readers and meet with book clubs. She'd love to hear from you, and personally answers every email that's sent to Zuri@ZuriDay.com.

CHAMPAGNE *Kisses*

ZURI DAY

Of diamond dreams and champagne kisses,
Can one really have that which one wishes?
I say yes, it's up to you…
To believe and act to make these dreams come true.

ISBN-13: 978-0-373-86278-8

CHAMPAGNE KISSES

Copyright © 2012 by Zuri Day

PLEASE RECYCLE
THIS PRODUCT IS RECYCLABLE

Recycling programs
for this product may
not exist in your area.

For questions and comments about the quality of this book please contact us at CustomerService@Harlequin.com.

www.Harlequin.com

Printed in U.S.A.

Dear Reader,

Do you know the history of champagne, how it is created through the second fermentation of the grape, which produces carbonation? Or how originally only the sparkling wine produced in the French region of Champagne was legally permitted to label their drink as such, which is the reason some popular labels to this day refer to their bubbly as "sparkling wine"?

Thanks to the Benedictine Monks in the Abbey of Saint Hilaire, near Carcassonne, who in 1531 filled their spare time creating a drink that calmed the mind as well as quenched the thirst, we enjoy a drink often associated with milestones and celebrations.

So please join me as I raise my glass in a toast to Donovan Drake, an heir to Drake Wines Resort & Spa, and Marissa Hayes, the woman Papa Dee calls "his even change." I believe that you'll feel as I do…they deserve each other's love!

Zuri Day

Thank you, Glenda Howard! You know why.
And Samuel Lewis…you know why, too!

Chapter 1

Four months earlier

"Let's go down the road and have a drink." Drake Wines Resort and Spa co-owner and executive, thirty-two-year-old Donovan Drake, eyed his prey with a serious expression, barely stopping himself from licking his lips and releasing a groan in anticipation of how the evening might end. That was if he had his way.

His target's eyes twinkled with humor as she contemplated the remark. "You're asking me to leave one of Southern California's most coveted resorts—" she waved her hand around the room "—featuring award-winning vineyards, to go somewhere *else* for a glass of wine?" Donovan smiled. The woman sitting across from him had a point. For the fifth year in a row, an assortment of Drake Wines had placed first in several categories at the Monterey Wine Festival, the California Beer and Wine Festival, the Vancouver Playhouse International Wine Festival and the Food and Wine Classic in Aspen, Colorado. The latter had led to an unprecedented six-page spread in the prestigious *Food and Wine Magazine,* a fact that had delighted his sister and director of PR, Diamond, whose wedding announcement and subsequent celebration had placed him near this dark-chocolate morsel.

"You're right, of course. There are no better wines than those in our vineyard. But when it comes to privacy, and particularly when it comes to not having the one-and-only Genevieve Drake, otherwise known as my mother, all up in my affairs, that is something else entirely."

"We're just talking. Why would you care if your mother sees that?"

"Because I'm male and you're female. That alone makes you immediately of interest where my mother is concerned." Marissa Hayes's look was a mix of mild confusion and skepticism. "She sees every woman her sons entertain, even in conversation, as potential marriage material. If we stay here it won't be long before she waltzes over to begin her informal interrogation."

"That is not how she appeared during the introductions," Marissa countered. "In fact, considering the force of the Drake name in the wine industry and beyond, and given Diamond's vivacious personality, I was surprised at how soft-spoken and laid-back she seems to be."

"Don't let those genteel manners and the velvet glove fool you. There's an iron fist shielded inside it and a shrewd, calculating mind behind that soft smile."

Marissa fiddled with one of her curly black locks as she took in the scenery, discreetly searching for the classy lady she'd learned was Donovan, Diamond and their younger brother Dexter's mom. While doing so, she also took in the well-appointed great room ensconced within the luxurious walls of the Drake estate; its soft ivory silk was a perfect backdrop to the velvet-covered chaises, brocade wingbacks and low-slung sectional clothed in antique damask. The ebony and ivory keys of the baby grand anchoring the other end of the room were being tickled by a very capable pianist. The nimble fingers of the young blonde who'd been introduced as a former prodigy effortlessly blended yesterday's sounds of Duke and Ella with today's George Benson, Kenny G and Esperanza Spalding. When she shifted her eyes from the piano player, they landed on Donovan's mother, a vision of sophistication in burgundy silk and silver accessories. She turned her head slightly toward Donovan and lifted her champagne flute. "I'm afraid you may be right, Mr. Drake. We're getting ready to have company."

Donovan didn't have to turn around to know who was approaching. Genevieve Drake had spotted them and was making the proverbial beeline for a closer examination of the woman who had held the attention of her son for longer than five minutes.

"Ah, there you are!" Genevieve Drake's carriage was one of pride and confidence as she reached her son and stepped in for a hug. A refined-looking lady with strong, vibrant features, long black hair streaked with gray and a slim, short frame, she exuded maternal comfort even as subtle hints of fire came through. "I think Keely did a fabulous job, don't you?"

"I do," Donovan said, looking around and raising his glass to Dexter, his perpetual-playboy brother holding court amid a circle of lovelies on the other side of the room. "But then again, we'd expect nothing less of Kathleen's daughter."

"Indeed."

Kathleen Fitzpatrick was a longtime Drake employee whose fire was less like subtle flickers and more like a burning flame. She'd begun her employ more than twenty-five years ago, working in various capacities based on need. For the past several years she'd worked in the PR and marketing department as Donovan's sister Diamond's assistant. Fiercely loyal and all about family, she'd been delighted when Diamond decided to hire her up-and-coming party-planner daughter for the fete to celebrate her highly talked about engagement to construction mogul Jackson "Boss" Wright. With a nod to the month and the moment, Keely's theme had revolved around hearts, with the symbol showing up in unique and creative ways around the room: ice sculptures; ice cubes; floral centerpieces; and, Genevieve's favorite, the keepsake candles that would go home with each guest. The color palette boasted almost every shade of red imaginable and, paired with champagne, was at once elegant and festive.

Genevieve turned to Marissa. "Hello, dear. I'm Donovan's mother, Genevieve Drake."

Marissa stuck out her hand. "Marissa Hayes. Mrs. Drake, it's a pleasure."

"The pleasure is mine." Genevieve reached for Marissa's hand only to pull her in for a hug. "We hug where I'm from," she said with a smile.

"Oh? And where's that?"

"The South. Louisiana. What about you, dear. From where does your family hail? With that beautiful brown skin, those high cheekbones and almond-shaped eyes, I'd probably lean toward the islands. Would I be wrong?"

"We all landed stateside as far as I know. I was born and raised in San Diego, ma'am, where I still live." Marissa suppressed a smile as she felt a subtle tug on her dress. She was sure it was Donovan's way of alerting her that Detective Genevieve's interrogation had begun.

"And your parents, they still live in San Diego as well?"

"No. My father is a minister who a few years ago was asked to become senior pastor of a prominent church in Chicago. They live just outside the Windy City in a suburb called Naperville."

Genevieve nodded. "I've heard of it, but have not been there. In fact, it's been years since I've visited the Midwest, including Chicago. I do love their deep-dish pizza. Donovan, what was the name of the restaurant we visited, what, ten years ago?"

"I don't remember, Mom. But speaking of food, Marissa and I were—"

"Oh, it doesn't matter," Genevieve went on. She did a surreptitious sweep of Marissa from head to toe. "Of course, with your stunning hourglass figure, you probably stay away from such calorie-laden treats."

"Probably not as much as I should."

"Hmm. I must say it is wonderful to talk with someone without having to look up continually. All of my children took after their father in that regard. What are you, five-three, four?"

"Okay, Mom. Let's not continue this round of twenty questions."

"How else does one get to know their guests?" Genevieve asked dryly with raised brow.

Marissa chuckled. "Really, Donovan. It's okay." Looking at Genevieve, she continued, "I understand completely. I'm five foot four and also the shortest one in my family, not counting my cousins or my nephew, who just turned two."

"Ha!" Genevieve's twinkling eyes signaled how much she was enjoying the conversation. "So you have siblings."

"A brother, who is older than me. He and his family live in Baltimore, Maryland, where his wife is from."

Donovan cleared his throat. Marissa hid another smile behind a sip of sparkling chardonnay, a Drake Wines favorite. Genevieve barreled on determinedly. "How do you know Diamond, dear?"

"I haven't had the pleasure of really getting to know her yet. I work for Boss Wright as his executive assistant."

"Really?" Genevieve didn't try to hide her surprise or heightened interest. "How long have you worked for him?"

"Okay, Mom. I think that's enough for one evening."

"I'm simply curious that someone as beautiful as this young lady didn't try and snap up one of the country's most eligible bachelors for herself." She turned still-sparkling eyes on Marissa and lowered her voice as if they were two longtime pals. "Or did you?" She winked, letting Marissa know that she was teasing, and continued talking, as if trying to get under her eldest son's skin.

It was working.

Donovan didn't think for one minute that his shrewd

mother was joking. He believed he knew the questions his mother wasn't asking: Had Marissa ever been interested in Jackson Wright? Had Jackson ever been interested in Marissa? Had Jackson and Marissa ever slept together? If so, why? If not, why? Was Donovan interested in Marissa? And if so, how fast could Genevieve do a background check?

"You know what they say about curiosity," Donovan drawled, gently taking his mother's shoulders and steering her away from Marissa. "It killed the cat." He kissed her on the top of her head. "We're going to check out the dessert buffet," he offered, to keep his mother from feeling totally dismissed.

"Enjoy your evening," Genevieve said over her shoulder to Marissa. "We'll talk again."

After Donovan had deposited Genevieve into the safe and capable hands of his father, Donald, he returned to where Marissa still stood. "Now you understand why I want to sample another vineyard's wines."

"Completely."

"So what do you say? Inland Empire Winery, Rancho California Road, fifteen minutes?"

Marissa smiled, and gave a nod. "I'll meet you there."

Chapter 2

Donovan watched Marissa wind her way through the crowd and over to where Jackson and Diamond stood. Later, he'd explain to his sis and brother-in-law-to-be why he didn't make his proper goodbyes. Diamond would understand. As with the brothers, she too had borne the brunt of Genevieve's desire to expand the clan and bounce grandchildren on her knee as soon as possible. One would think that with Diamond's wedding on the horizon the pressure would have lessened. Instead, her impending nuptials had created the opposite effect, especially where he was concerned.

"You're the oldest," Genevieve had chided the morning after Jackson proposed to Diamond. "I never thought I'd see the day where your sister beat you at anything." Despite their competitive nature, this was one race Donovan had gladly lost to a sibling. He'd happily get beaten by Dexter, too, though hell would have probably frozen over and Armageddon made itself known before baby brother ended his Don Juan ways. In an attempt to throw off an undoubtedly still curious Genevieve from his trail, Donovan walked in the opposite direction as Marissa, joining his brother and the circle of female admirers that surrounded him. After another minute or two, he slipped out a side door, doubled back through the garden, around the infinity pool and into the parking lot. Bypassing his Mercedes—because if she noticed his car missing Detective Genevieve would undoubtedly ask what type of car Marissa owned—he walked the cobblestoned path to the company garage and settled into a company car. After retrieving the car keys that were always stowed in the overhead visor, he eased the Lexus hybrid out of the garage and was on his way.

The night was cool and the stars bright and vibrant as he made his way down the private winding road of the Drake Resort before turning left onto Rancho California Road and the short drive to his destination. He reached the neighboring winery, with which the Drakes maintained a friendly rivalry; parked near the front; and, bypassing the restaurant, opted for the less formal tasting bar. On this, the Saturday before Valentine's Day, it was only moderately crowded. The bartender greeted Donovan by name, served up a deep-bodied cabernet franc and placed a bowl of salty nuts and pretzels within easy reach. After allowing a moment for the wine to breathe, Donovan picked up the glass, swirled its contents and thought of Marissa Hayes.

He'd noticed her the moment she'd arrived at the party. He'd seen the delicious smile she gave the valet as she exited her car and received her ticket. Donovan had been standing near the door, having just returned from escorting his great-grandfather—the family patriarch—from the north wing of the ten-thousand-square-foot home to where the festivities were being held. David Drake, Sr., a ninety-nine-year-young fountain of ever-spouting wisdom, whom everyone fondly called Papa Dee, had noticed her, too. His surprisingly clear eyes had gleamed with mischief when he said, "That's a fine filly there, Donovan. An old man won't fault you for abandoning me in favor of taking that youngling for a ride." Donovan had laughed off the comment, but the short, stacked, brown bombshell rocking the forest-green, velvety-looking dress and stiletto heels had not only captured his attention, but she maintained it throughout the course of the evening.

He knew who she was, had remembered her from a few months earlier and the gala that celebrated the official opening of Drake Wines Resort and Spa. That's how Diamond had become acquainted with Jackson, when his construction company, Boss Construction, won the bid to transform the twenty-five-year-old facility. It had been totally renovated and expanded to include a boutique hotel with a separate honeymoon house on the hill, a stand-alone gift shop and wine store and a world-class spa offering everything from massages to mud baths along with a full-service salon. All of this sat on more than five hundred acres of rolling hills and sterling grapevines. It was set against the mountainous backdrop of Temecula, a perfect place for weddings and the site for his sister's upcoming nuptials.

His interest had been piqued that first time he'd seen Marissa, and he recalled the way his heart had clenched at the sight of her while something decidedly lower had also bobbed its amen. He remembered the way she'd offered a coy smile before glancing away from his intense gaze and how a jolt of electricity had accompanied their handshake. Most important he remembered the way that no matter how hard he tried all evening, he seemed to not be able to corner her; less than an hour into the party he'd found out she'd already left. Something about an upset stomach, Jackson had said. Upon finding out that she was gone, he'd shrugged off the attraction, hadn't given her a second thought. Until tonight. But ever since he'd seen her tonight, he knew that her slipping through his fingers again was not an option. Not the way she was swinging that hair and wearing that dress, with a body so vivacious it should have come with a warning sign. *Dangerous Curves Ahead.*

Donovan looked at his Rolex and then watched as the brother who was also at the bar finished his drink and passed a business card to the blonde seated between them before he walked out the door. The blonde turned to Donovan.

"What a jerk," she said as she tore the business card in half before offering him a flirty look. Donovan gave her an understanding smile before turning his chair to face the bar's liquor-covered shelves. He was sympathetic but not interested. Not tonight anyway. It had now been twenty minutes since Marissa had promised to meet him in fifteen. Leaning back in the comfy bar chair, he took another slow, deliberate sip of wine. His mother had taught him that anything worth having was worth waiting for. Donovan Drake was nothing if not a patient man.

* * *

Marissa pulled into the parking lot, her heart thumping with excitement. It seemed forever ago that she'd even consider giving a man her phone number, let alone meeting one for a drink. Her employer, Jackson, and anyone else who knew her would consider the night's actions quite unlike her. But there was something about Donovan Drake that seemed different from the average man, something that made her feel safe and protected. He exuded a type of authority that you could only be born with, yet had a way of making you feel comfortable in his presence. Oh, and there was that minor detail about him being very good-looking. Not in a pretty-boy way like Trey Songz or Boris Kodjoe, or even in a *Dayum!* sort of fashion like his tall, hunky brother, Dexter. No, Donovan's good looks were as much from what was within as the package without.

This is why she'd ignored the fact that at the moment, she wasn't supposed to be interested in the opposite sex, that after the betrayal she'd endured from a so-called friend, work and continuing her education were the only two things that were supposed to have her attention. But the smile currently on her face had nothing to do with executive assistant work or landing a graduate degree in business administration, and everything to do with a tall, strapping male, one she'd thought of intermittently since being introduced to him months before. Then, as now, there had been nothing about the six-foot-tall, broad-shouldered sculpture of brown sugar that she hadn't liked. Not his smoldering cocoa eyes, his juicy lips, his wide, thick eyebrows or that hint of a cleft that kissed the middle of a strong jawline. Nothing. This was probably why her heart raced as though she was on a first date. She felt she could fall in like with Donovan Drake very easily. She'd already fallen in lust.

"Let's go, Marissa," she encouraged herself. "It's only a drink." With one last look in the mirror and a quick sprucing up of her curly, shoulder-length tresses, Marissa got out of the car, got halfway between the parking lot and the tasting room door…and froze.

"Well, well, well."

Thump, thump. Thump, thump. Her heartbeat was so loud it almost drowned out the voice she'd hoped to never hear again. At least not for a few lifetimes. Unfortunately this pitter-patter had nothing to do with the man for whom she lusted and everything to do with one she despised.

"Hello, Marissa."

Figuring the faster she'd speak, the faster he'd leave, her lips parted. "Hello, Steven."

"You're looking good."

Any comment she would have offered, if it existed, would have had a hard time squeezing past the tightness in her throat. The greeting had been hard enough.

Steven eyed her a moment longer before turning to look through the window at the wall-length bar just beyond them. Marissa immediately saw Donovan talking to the bartender. On one side of him was a tanned man with dark hair and a mustache; a blonde woman sat on his other side. A couple walked up and took two seats on the short side of the L-shaped counter. "Which one of them are you here to meet?"

Marissa swallowed her discomfort, squared her shoulders and tried to not show how totally uncomfortable she was seeing her former best friend again.

"I've purposely stayed away from Long Beach and

certain areas of San Diego so that I don't have to see you. And now, I find you conveniently in between the two at the exact same time as I am. Are you stalking me?"

Steven laughed, the sound sinister and hollow. When he replied, his eyes were cold. "Don't flatter yourself."

"Then how did you find me, Steven?"

"I wasn't looking for you. Antonio's band has a gig out this way. Not that it's any of your business." They continued eyeing each other a moment. "I see you still believe that bull those strangers told you."

"That's right. I still believe it. And I still meant what I said when it happened. If I have another confrontation with you, if you harass me in any way, I will get a restraining order."

Steven shrugged. "You do whatever you feel you need to do. Handle your business, because I'm definitely going to handle mine."

Marissa took a deep breath and tried another *approach.* "You know what, Steven? Somewhere inside you is a nice person. I knew him once. In fact, we used to be friends."

"That good man is still right here," Steven said with that boyish smile Marissa remembered. "In fact, that good man still wants to take our relationship to the next level. I've already seen you," he said cockily, with a long, lascivious visual sweep of her body. "Might as well let me tap that—"

"That's enough," Marissa hissed between gritted teeth. She found the nerve of this former best friend infuriating. She wanted to lash out, curse him out. Remembering the darker moments of their shared history, she chose to stay calm and keep her wits about her.

And just in time, as it turned out.

"Which one of those jerks are you screwing?" Steven demanded, his brow creased in anger as he pointed toward the glass. "Which one did you offer on a silver platter what I couldn't beg you out of? I told you I'd deal with whoever came between us."

That's right. He had told her, that last night they were together, the night that changed everything. It was why she hadn't gone on a date in a very long time. It wasn't worth putting a potential new friend at risk. The Steven McCain she'd known since college had been smart, funny and trustworthy. Or so she'd thought. Until that fateful night he'd tried to take their friendship to another level. By any means necessary. That's when she'd begun to believe he might not be as nice as he'd seemed. Or as sane.

She looked from him to the window, saw Donovan glance at his watch. *Dang it, I don't even have Donovan's cell phone number.* But she had common sense, and she knew that to go in now, to get anywhere near Donovan, would not only result in an altercation, but would tell the lunatic standing in front of her more than he needed to know. Reluctantly, she turned back to her car. "Stay away from me, Steven," she threw over her shoulder.

"My phone number is the same, Marissa, and you need to use it. Let's get together, just to talk, I promise." She kept on walking. "Remember I can blow the cover on that goody-two-shoes image you're boasting."

Marissa ignored him, got into her car, started the engine and sped away.

Donovan was getting just a bit antsy. Not at the fact that he might have been stood up, no, he'd seen the look of interest in Marissa's eyes. And more than that, for some reason he felt she was a woman of her word. He definitely knew what the other type of woman looked like, the one who would say one thing and do another, the one who wouldn't know the meaning of such words as honor, truth or integrity unless looked up in a dictionary. It had been a half hour since they'd parted. Should he entertain the remote possibility that she'd gotten into an accident? It seemed unlikely considering the short distance she would have traveled. Or could it be something much more likely, such as her having been sidetracked by someone at the party, like his mother?

Donovan's eyes shifted from the window to the door, and he noticed the cocky-looking dude who'd been flirting with—translated, harassing—the cute blonde at the end of the bar watching a pair of taillights speed out of the parking lot. The man watched the car, a silver sporty number, as it turned onto the street, all the way until it was out of sight. Then he confidently walked to his black sedan and sped off, as well.

Donovan turned back to the bar and finished his wine. Then he reached for his phone and called his soon-to-be brother-in-law. "Boss, it's Donovan. I'm looking for Marissa."

"She's not with you?"

"No. I thought she might have gotten sidetracked and was talking to either my mother or Diamond."

"No, man, she left about fifteen, twenty minutes ago. She mentioned meeting you and told me she'd see me in the morning."

An uncomfortable feeling came over Donovan as he turned back toward the parking lot. The scene he'd just witnessed replayed in his mind. "What kind of car does she drive?"

"A little two-door Honda Civic."

"What color?"

"Silver, why?"

"Because I…never mind."

"Donovan, wait—"

But he didn't. Donovan ended the call, paid the tab and left the establishment. He'd bet money that it was Marissa's car he'd seen leave the parking lot and figured that she knew the cocky dude no doubt now hot on her trail. The identity of the man was not important, nor did Donovan care what business Marissa had with him. The only thing that was important was the fact that she'd left without coming in to see him.

There was one thought on Donovan's mind as he thanked the bartender who'd waved away his attempt to pay him. One thought as he exited the establishment, tightened his collar against the cool air and walked to his car. *How could I have so misjudged her?* He would have bet money that Marissa Hayes was not fickle or shallow like so many of the women Dexter dated, and totally unlike the last woman he'd trusted with his heart. He would have bet money, big money.

Yes, and you would have lost.

Chapter 3

Four months later

The private room at Grapevine, the upscale restaurant at Drake Wines Resort and Spa, bustled with activity. The excitement in the air was almost tangible. Waiters went to and from the kitchen carrying trays of succulent appetizers: truffle-infused macaroni and cheese balls, lamb-stuffed mushroom caps, salmon satays, vegetable kebabs, pecan-crusted shrimp on a stick and breaded parmesan artichoke hearts. Conversation flowed as smoothly as the wine. A mixture of instrumental music—jazz, classical and R & B—provided a nonintrusive backdrop, and the four-dozen guests enjoying the evening were as beautiful as the freshly cut calla lilies that graced each table's centerpiece.

"You know what's so amazing?" Jackson walked up

to his soon-to-be brother-in-law and stood beside him. "She's as beautiful a person on the inside as she is on the outside."

A crease of frustration crossed Donovan's brow. "Who?"

Jackson chuckled.

Instead of responding to the obvious taunt, Donovan turned his head away from the vixen across the room. If only his lower head would follow suit and stop twitching like a snake after a shiny red apple. Even though said "apple" filled out the back of the navy slacks she wore to perfection. He'd tried once before with Jackson's executive assistant, the lovely Marissa Hayes, and while she'd finally explained why she'd arrived at the Inland Empire tasting room but hadn't come inside, he'd still taken it as a sign to back off. He need look no further than his younger brother to see the kind of drama that could accompany an attractive woman. Dexter thrived on that type of foolishness. Donovan, not so much.

Which is why when he needed a particular itch scratched, there was a nice, widowed woman in San Diego to do the job. Straightforward, uncomplicated, that had been their arrangement. Each had grown-up needs, and neither was looking for more than physical fulfillment and occasional company. Or at least that's how it had been until five months ago when Ms. Widowed had joined a dating website, met a man and moved to Cleveland. Donovan had intended to find a replacement, but the company's latest project, a major expansion that would introduce high-end Drake Wines to an upscale Asian market and then, if successful, to the rest of the world had thrown his schedule into a tizzy and put Donovan into a prolonged period of unintended abstinence.

When he'd seen Marissa, truth be told, he'd been more than ready to get back in the sexual game. He didn't even want to think about why, since meeting one certain curvy cutie on that fateful night in February, he couldn't seem to develop an interest in any other female. The international expansion had provided the positive jolt he needed. Not only was the company developing a line of high-end wines specifically for this market, but during the holidays they were finally going to unveil an exclusive champagne that Dexter, under the watchful eye and guidance of his mentor, Papa Dee, had been working on for many years. And finally, there was the partnership that the Drakes of California had entered into with their cousins, the Drakes of Louisiana. This family of six sons had made their name in the world of real estate and had broken into the Asian market five years ago. One of their latest successes was a line of trendy wine bars that, as of next year, would feature an exclusive line of Drake Wines, including the new champagne. As busy as the year had been so far, the next six months were going to be even busier. Donovan was glad there was no time for a relationship, but wasn't too appreciative of the booty that kept reminding him it was past time for something else.

"Why don't you take my advice and go talk to her?" Jackson stared straight ahead, too, a slight smile belying the seriousness of his tone. It wasn't often that he saw The Don rattled.

"Man, I don't know what you're talking about," Donovan said, finally cutting his eyes in Jackson's direction.

"You might not know what I'm talking about. But you definitely know *who* I'm talking about."

"There are eight women in that circle on the other side of the room. Why do you think I'm looking at Marissa?"

Jackson laughed out loud. "That's why!"

Donovan shook his head and forced his eyes away from one of his sister's bridesmaids and Jackson's assistant; he turned to face Jackson directly. "I know you and Diamond are set on matchmaking, but you know your girl stood me up, right?" Donovan hurried on when Jackson would have argued. "She didn't meet me because something, or more specifically someone, came up. But the fact that she wouldn't offer any explanation as to why his seeing her with me would have been a problem, after telling me that this guy wasn't an ex-boyfriend but an ex-friend?" Donovan shook his head. "It's just too strange and complicated for me, you know? Besides, I have enough on my plate right now." He observed Jackson's doubtful expression. "Really, I'm good."

"Yeah, well, you should let your face know," was Jackson's dry retort. "Because when I see you look at Marissa…your face tells a different story."

Donovan turned and walked away. Since Jackson was such an expert at interpreting body language, he figured that the "I'm done with this conversation" move would be an easy read. Through three courses he continued to brood. Deciding to skip dessert, he nodded at a couple of the groomsmen as he made his way from the private dining room where the rehearsal dinner was being held to the veranda beyond it. He opened the door, stepped out into the warm wrap of a June evening and inhaled his mother's contribution to the resort's design: gardenia, jasmine and honeysuckle flowers climbing up arbors, clinging to lattices and lining the planters that ran the length of the porch. The sky was clear, with brilliant stars shining like diamonds against an inky sky. One of the things he loved about the sky over Temecula was how the shades of blue played off of one another long into the night. Even now, at almost ten o'clock and with the sun long since having bid its adieu for the evening, earth's ceiling did not strike a monochromatic chord. The sky was streaked with shades of blue, and wisps of nearly transparent clouds added a hazy, almost surreal quality to the night. Donovan peered at the sky, the deep, deep blue and thought of…navy slacks and plump behinds and how he'd like to—

Buzz.

Thankful for the interruption, Donovan quickly fished his cell phone from his slacks and checked the ID. "Hello, Sharon. This is a surprise. What are you doing up so late?" Donovan's longtime assistant Sharon Brockman's early bedtime ritual was a running joke between them. If she were up past ten o'clock, weekday or weekend, it was a late night.

"Donovan, I'm in the hospital."

"Oh, no, Sharon. I'm so sorry to hear that." And he was, for many reasons. Like Kathleen Fitzpatrick, Sharon had worked at the vineyard for years, almost from the beginning. She was less an employee and more a member of the family. "What happened?"

"The pain came back, but stronger this time. They just ran a battery of tests on me and, Donovan, I'm afraid that my coming back to work on Monday doesn't look good. The doctors think I'll likely have to have surgery. I know we were trying to avoid that, or at least put it off until sometime next month, but my body isn't cooperating."

As much as he needed his assistant right now, Donovan was immediately concerned more about Sharon's welfare and less about how her absence would affect the company's productivity. When she'd felt the sharp pain a couple days ago, Sharon had told him she thought it was an embarrassing case of internal hemorrhoids, something she'd dealt with off and on since having her now-grown children. She'd taken over-the-counter medicines and, with the help of prescription-strength aspirin, had come back to work the next day saying she was as good as new. Obviously, that was not the case.

Donovan's voice was laced with concern. "Do they know what it is?"

"A colon tear, brought on by an infection that I didn't know I had. I'm so sorry."

"Don't even think about apologizing for something you can't control. The main concern here is you getting better. I don't want you to focus on anything but that."

"But the project. I know how you feel about the confidential nature—"

"Don't worry about it. Sharon, I'm serious. There's nothing more important than your getting well. We'll be okay here until you get back."

"How does one's colon's tear anyway?"

An inquisitive mind, a love for research and attention to detail were just a few of the qualities that made Sharon a top-notch assistant. "I'm sure that before you leave that hospital, you'll know at least as much about what's going on as the doctor."

"Donovan, my daughter is rushing me off the phone.

Because of her, I'll probably feel more pain in the you-know-what than if I had hemorrhoids!"

"Ha! Give Patrice my phone number so that during your surgery she can keep me updated. And I meant what I said, Sharon. Don't worry about work—we'll be fine. Focus on getting better."

Donovan ended the call and then heaved a sigh. Talk about bad timing. A couple unplanned sales trips, not to mention his increased jaunts to Louisiana, plus the festivities surrounding Diamond's wedding had put him way behind. They were all part of the reason the Herculean task of setting up the database and then inputting the more than ten thousand potential customers for this group of exclusive wines, plus marking out business partners and naming the product—all tasks requiring the utmost confidentiality—had been pushed back to the two-week period following the wedding when the resort had calmed back down. This delay, and another inevitable interruption, otherwise known as the upcoming Fourth of July holiday, and he was pushed right up against an unmovable timeline. Attorneys, accountants, consultants and other participating third parties were all lined up, waiting and ready to put their piece of this new financially rewarding puzzle in place.

Dammit!

"Wow, it's beautiful out here." Donovan closed his eyes against the sound of the woman that Sharon's call had helped put out of his mind. Marissa stood beside him as he leaned across the railing. "Do you mind if I join you?"

"It's public property," Donovan replied huffily. He pushed off of the railing, stuffed his hands in his pocket and moved away a couple feet.

Marissa eyed his actions in slight amazement. Was he really still simmering over what happened months ago? That she hadn't shown up for a lousy glass of wine? She'd told him that she'd arrived at the bar and she'd told him why she had left. What else did he want from her? An apology written in blood?

The rehearsal dinner was over so the logical thing for Marissa to do was to turn around without another word and head back to the peace and quiet of her San Diego apartment. But logic had obviously gone on vacation and its nemesis, crazy, was calling the shots. So Marissa pressed forward. "The rehearsal dinner went well, and the hill is such a perfect place for the ceremony. Diamond's wedding is going to be lovely."

His silence was deafening.

"I would wonder whether or not you've been taught manners, but since I've met your mother, I know that answer is yes. So I can only assume you're being a jerk, still smarting over a slight that happened months ago." Nothing moved on the veranda, not even the wind. "I can be ignored by you all night." *How well I'm dealing with it is another story altogether.* There hadn't been a moment all evening when Marissa hadn't been aware of Donovan's presence, how good he looked as Jackson's best man and how much he was admired by the other women. "Your sister is marrying my boss, which means our paths may cross on occasion. I don't think being civil is too much to ask."

Donovan wheeled around in a manner so uncharacteristic that Marissa took a step back. "So I'm supposed to care about what you think?" The words came out in clipped fashion; his voice was low, almost too calm.

Later, Marissa would wonder at her uncharacteristically flippant response. "You can do what you want. But I'd think that someone of your intelligence would understand when a situation is untenable. As I stated before, given who I met in the parking lot, coming in to meet you in the restaurant would have been a problem."

"You think you're the only one who's had a problem with the opposite sex? You don't get to corner the market on bad situations, and I don't have to engage you in friendly conversation." The words hit their mark; evidenced by the frozen expression on Marissa's face and the hurt look in her eyes. "Look, Marissa, I'm sorry to snap at you. I've got a lot on my mind."

"And you obviously need a lot of room to think about all of what's on there. I'll leave you to it." The click-clack of her heels sounded as she made quick work of the distance between the veranda's edge and the door. Going after her was not an option. Not only would that capture every Drakes' attention within a one-mile radius but he wouldn't have a clue of what to say about his brutish behavior. Obviously, he'd said too much already.

Chapter 4

The female guests had been asked to wear designs in predominate shades of purple or blue, meant to complement the brilliant cobalt sky of a picture-perfect summer day. The men had been told to dress in casual suits, shades of tan, beige or ivory preferred. Wanting her wedding to be visually coordinated in these hues, the color black had been highly discouraged. Okay, banned. All two hundred guests had complied, causing the people bouquet to match the appropriately tinted flowers: tie-dyed dendrobium orchids, irises, anemones, hydrangea, roses and million star baby's breath. The bridesmaids wore various shades of blue or tan while the maid of honor's dress was a rich, deep navy, which matched the best man's suit. The groomsmen carried on the tan/beige/ivory theme, a nod to the mounds surrounding the golf course and the stone pathways that could be seen from the hill. Kathleen Fitzpatrick's granddaughter was the flower girl, a redheaded bundle of fluffy baby-blue organza. The maid of honor's ivory-suited son bore the rings. Both Diamond and Jackson wore dazzling white, and they looked not only amazing, but ridiculously in love. The tearjerker had been when three generations of Drakes—Diamond's father, Donald; her grandfather David, Jr.; and her great-grandfather, David, Sr.— walked her down the aisle. The comic relief had come when Papa Dee nudged Jackson, tilted his head toward Diamond and said, "That's one feisty filly. Best watch yourself." No matter that the loudly whispered suggestion was only heard by the first two rows. It became the most repeated statement of the day. *Best watch yourself.* The temperature had been a forgiving seventy-two degrees; the greenery of the vineyard and surrounding lawns had wrapped all of them in nature's flawless tranquility.

It was, quite simply, the most beautiful wedding Marissa had ever witnessed. That she'd gotten to see it all from the position of bridesmaid, and given the fact that Diamond's large wedding entourage had made her role one mostly of administrative support, Marissa should have been almost as happy as the bride. But she wasn't. Even now, the smile she wore was as pasted on as the tail of the donkey at a six-year-old's birthday party. The banter she'd kept up for Diamond's sake as they rode in the pimped-out golf cart (white tulle, Swarovski-encrusted canopied top, spinning hubcaps—yes, on a golf cart) that whisked them from the gazebo-covered hilltop to the dress change awaiting in the main house, was more to stifle her own thoughts than to ensure Diamond's continued good mood.

Bottom line? Marissa was masking an emotional odor that stank to high heavens. She was, simply stated, in a funk.

Anyone watching would have had to admit she was nothing if not a trouper, prattling on while working to not become engulfed in the endless yards of Diamond's puffy chiffon, twenty-foot court train. It didn't matter that Diamond and her brand-new husband, Jackson, were riding in the middle row of the six-seater golf cart, directly in front of her. The train's presence was *everywhere*. "Your great-grandfather was so funny, and his more seriously delivered words of wisdom were amazing," Marissa continued, maneuvering the train and talking as if her voice would disappear if the words stopped. "What he said about the long slow walk beating a fast sprint any day—" she chuckled "—everyone listening knew exactly what that meant! I can't believe that he's almost a hundred years old. He doesn't look a day over eighty, seventy even." Even in her frazzled state of mind she thought that saying someone looked eighty didn't sound good, even though she'd just shaved twenty years off someone's existence. "Well, what I meant to say was—"

"It's all right, Marissa," Diamond said, her hand in midair to ward off the oratorical flow. "And I don't mean to be rude. I just need to gather my thoughts and…" The sentence died on Diamond's lips as Jackson placed his arm around her shoulders.

"Of course." Marissa looked between her boss and Diamond and for the first time noticed a strain on her face. Considering how flawless the ceremony had gone, and given the meticulous organization of the upcoming dinner and dance, what was there to be worried about?

"I'm sorry, girl, going on and on like that." Jackson gave an almost imperceptible nod, one that Marissa caught only because he'd been her employer for several years. His expression prompted her to ask the question that must have shown in her eyes. Her voice lowered to a near whisper as she looked at Diamond. "What's wrong?" She noticed Diamond's deep breath, and she could have sworn that tears also threatened. "What is it?" Marissa asked again with growing concern.

"We received some troubling news last night. One of our employees had emergency surgery and is in very critical condition."

Marissa placed a hand on her friend's arm. "I'm so sorry, Diamond. Was it someone who works in the PR department?"

Diamond shook her head. "It's Donovan's assistant. Sharon has been with the company for twenty years. She's like family to us all."

Donovan's assistant. Like family. That's what was wrong last night. The reason he'd been quiet after the rehearsal dinner, and so withdrawn… No wonder he'd lashed out at her. *I'm sorry to snap at you. I've got a lot on my mind.*

By the time she'd rounded the golf cart to help Diamond and the maid of honor with the gargantuan train, four more carts had pulled up behind them. Her personal assistant for the day, a young college intern working in PR for the summer, jumped out of the cart and was at Diamond's side in an instant. Jackson shooed him away as he turned, lifted Diamond from the cart and deftly placed her on the ground. The rest of the wedding entourage, including Diamond's stylist, hairdresser and makeup artist, all began walking toward the building where Diamond would change into her second dress. It was a good thing that there were so many people to help, leaving any assistance needed from Marissa to be minimal at best. Because all she could think about was Donovan and how unfairly she'd treated him.

She'd been so quick to lump him into the jerk category with the rest of the men she'd recently encountered when nothing could have been further from the truth. The eldest Drake sibling was just as she'd first believed him to be: considerate and thoughtful, and now she could add caring. He'd been preoccupied with his concern for someone else, someone who wasn't even a family member but a longtime employee. It's how Jackson would have reacted, with fierce loyalty and unwavering focus. That's because her boss, Jackson Wright, was a good man. Now, she was convinced that the same was true of Donovan Drake. And before the end of the day, come hell or high water, she was going to let him know how she felt.

Chapter 5

"That was a beautiful toast, brother," Jackson said once Donovan had taken his seat and the applause had subsided. They were seated on a raised dais facing the wedding guests seated at round tables of ten.

"Meant every word. There was a time when I doubted whether or not you were good enough for my sister."

"And now?"

"Couldn't find a better brother." Donovan felt his phone vibrate. His body instantly tensed as he pulled it from his pocket and discreetly held it under the table as he read the message.

"Everything okay?" Jackson asked.

Donovan sighed. "Get Diamond's attention." Jackson tapped Diamond and gave her a kiss as she turned to face him. Her lips met Jackson's, but then her eyes were squarely on her brother. "Did they text you?"

Donovan nodded. "They are scheduling another surgery first thing tomorrow."

"On a Sunday?" Diamond sounded shocked. "Donovan, I totally understand if you need to leave and go to the hospital."

Donovan slowly nodded, knowing the strain of the situation was showing on his face.

"Oh, wow," Diamond continued, as if finally understanding the gravity of the entire situation. "Your project! You're supposed to be pulling it all together in the next two weeks."

"I know," Donovan said, hating to bring such a topic into their wedding celebration but knowing that Diamond totally understood.

"What are you going to do?"

"I don't know. I thought about asking Mama to help—"

Diamond released an unladylike snort. "Good luck with that." While Genevieve had worked in the offices during the first couple years, she'd been a stay-at-home and run-the-home mother for more than three decades.

"What about Marissa?" Jackson asked, looking at Donovan. After not getting an immediate answer, he swung his head toward his wife. "What do you think, baby? There isn't going to be anything major happening at my company while I'm away, and—" he turned and continued the thought with Donovan in his line of sight "—whatever your project entails, I'm sure Marissa can handle it. She's an intelligent woman who catches on quick and has a knack for breaking the big picture into manageable bites. You know what, Donovan? I like the idea. Your project is of a sensitive nature, and

I know that Marissa could be trusted with this confidential material. Right, baby?"

Diamond looked at her new husband with a smile. "No doubt. Marissa seems loyal to a fault."

A scowl passed across Jackson's face so quickly that Donovan thought he imagined it. "If you give her something to do, she'll get the job done."

Diamond took a sip of her champagne. "What do you say, brother? I think Jackson has suggested a solution to your problem, and, while we'll all not totally rest until Sharon is well, at least this part of your business will only be minimally affected."

Their conversation was interrupted as their father, Donald Drake, stood to make a toast. Several other toasts followed and the dinner service began. Halfway through the entrée, a delectable combination of Dungeness crab, Kobe beef tenderloin, Bhutanese rice and steamed vegetables, Jackson made a move that had it not been for the deliciousness of the food would have ruined Donovan's appetite. He requested a pen and pad from one of the floating waiters, then quickly scribbled ten numbers onto the sheet of Drake Resort stationery. Above the numbers was one word: Marissa. And without even thinking about it, Donovan knew that the number on that paper was a game changer. He didn't know the name of the game or the rules. But he knew who would be playing.

It was a shame to waste such delicious food, but Marissa couldn't get a bite of the tender beef or a spear of the perfectly steamed broccoli past the lump in her throat. Didn't matter. If she had, the food would have just collided with the knot in her stomach. She was

seated at a table with other bridesmaids and groomsmen, including Reginald, one of Donovan's first cousins, who'd been bugging her nonstop ever since they'd
been paired up for the walk down the aisle. He wasn't a
bad-looking guy. In fact, he was fine: tall, butterscotch
complexion, a pretty boy. Nice enough, too. Another
time, another day and she would have been interested.
But her thoughts, and eyes, kept shifting to Donovan,
who for better or worse was seated directly in her line
of vision. She'd watched as her boss conversed with
him and Diamond, and she'd also noticed when one of
the waiters was summoned. Unfortunately, Reginald,
the determined groomsmen from New Orleans, chose
this time to begin a lengthy conversation—translated,
monologue, because "ums" and head nods could hardly
be counted as contributions—about some type of business that was expanding in Asia that later, for the life
of her, Marissa would not be able to recall. She tried
to split her focus between what her tablemate was saying and what was happening on the dais beyond her
but Reginald asked her a question and by the time she
answered it and looked up, the waiter was leaving the
head table, Jackson was talking to Diamond and Donovan was sitting there with a frown on his face. *What
had happened?*

"Should I take your silence as a no?"

Marissa turned to Reginald. "I'm sorry, my mind—"
attention, interest, focus, you name it "—was elsewhere.
What did you say?"

"I asked if you'd ever attended the Essence Music
Festival."

"No, I haven't."

"But you've been to New Orleans before, right?"

"Actually, no." *And if there's a chance I'll run into your nonstop chatter, I probably won't make it down there anytime soon!* Marissa immediately felt bad at the thought. Considering that she'd been the oratorical fountain earlier in the day she really was one to, well, talk.

"You should. It's a very nice event. In fact, we should exchange phone numbers and keep in touch. Our family is quite involved in various entities of the city, and we get VIP tickets to all of the parties and the concerts, of course. Then there are the private affairs that happen around town. I know that place like the back of my hand, could walk the streets in my sleep. Especially the French Quarter with its hotels, clubs, restaurants and impromptu jam sessions all up and down Bourbon Street. Have you ever had a beignet? Because if you haven't, after you've tried one you'll never look at a donut the same again. They're crispy on the outside, light and fluffy on the inside and..."

Try as she might to be courteous and attentive, the rest of Reginald's conversation was a bunch of blah, blah, blah. Thankfully the toasts continued and shortly after they'd taken away the dessert plates, Diamond and Jackson were cutting the cake. Everyone spilled from their places at the tables to witness the traditional cutting and made room on the floor for the newlywed's first dance. This was the moment Marissa had been waiting for. In between Reginald's rambling, she'd thought of the perfect way to get Donovan to herself, have him close enough to let him know exactly what was on her mind. But when she mustered up the nerve and crossed over to where she'd last seen him...he was gone.

Chapter 6

"Good morning, son," Genevieve said, opening the front door and giving Donovan a hug as he entered. "This is a pleasant surprise."

Until yesterday's wedding, Diamond had lived in the east wing of the estate. Dexter's domain was on the west side of the house. His mother insisted on maintaining a room for her eldest on the property, even though four years ago Donovan had purchased a Mediterranean-style, ocean-view home in La Jolla, a tony suburb of San Diego that was about an hour from his parents. For the past two years, until Ms. Widowed had changed her zip code, he'd lived there almost exclusively. During that time, he was a frequent dinner guest at the Drake estate but was rarely seen for breakfast.

Therefore Donovan understood, even expected, her surprise. "Morning, Mom." He followed her into a sitting room where she'd obviously been having tea.

"Should I pour you a cup, darling? If you're hungry, there's plenty of the breakfast casserole left. That's what we had this morning."

"Tea sounds good."

After pouring the tea and, against Donovan's wishes, retrieving a plate of homemade pastries from the kitchen, Genevieve explained simply, "Your grandmother made these."

"Oh, well, I definitely can't turn down her cooking." Though internal stress over his assistant's condition and the current workweek had lessened his appetite, he reached for one of the cinnamon rolls, then closed his eyes as he chewed the heavenly goodness. "This is delicious."

"How is Sharon?" Genevieve asked as she stirred her tea. "Dexter told me that that was why you left early."

"Yes. I knew how frightened her daughter had to be waiting for family to arrive from back east. Diamond encouraged me to go, and it was the right thing to do."

"And how is she?"

"The surgery was a success, but she's going to remain in ICU until they can be sure that no additional infection has set in."

Genevieve nodded. "I'll call later this morning and, if she's up to it, go visit her tomorrow. If you haven't already, remember to send flowers. Speaking of, who's covering for Sharon while she recuperates?"

"A temporary agency is sending someone to handle the day-to-day. But there's so much going on with the international expansion. Dexter would normally pick up the slack, but he has his hands full with the cousins and developing the line for stocking their wine bars."

"Donald mentioned that these next couple weeks are

very crucial for you, Donovan. All the more reason why your visit this morning, with so much going on, is a surprise." After a companionable silence she continued, "What can I do for you, son?"

Now that he was here, the speech that Donovan had rehearsed in his mind seemed lame and the idea that precipitated this talk even lamer. But his trusted assistant was in the hospital and his back was against the wall. After a fitful night's sleep, he'd wavered in the decision to work with Marissa. As sound as the advice Jackson had given and Diamond had readily seconded was, Donovan knew that being around that cup of hot chocolate would be a major distraction, and, quite frankly, he wasn't sure he could maintain professionalism instead of trying to take a few sips. So with one last bite of Grandmother Mary's cinnamon roll for fortification, he began.

"I need your help, Mom, professionally."

"Professionally?" Genevieve repeated with an arched brow as she set down her cup.

"Yes. Our partners in Asia have a database of over ten thousand potential customers for our wines. Unfortunately, the data was input in Chinese and, while we have some software that will do the translation, we can't download their file directly from their system to ours. The entries will have to be done manually. Aside from Sharon, Kathleen would have been the only person I could have trusted, but unfortunately Diamond had already promised her this week off."

"Your back is against the wall for sure, son. But how can I help?"

"Mom," he said, looking her in the eye. "I'd like your help with the international project."

"You're asking me to be your assistant, Donovan? Inputting this data, these tens of thousands of companies?"

Hearing it from his mother's mouth, Donovan felt he had more of a chance of the First Lady coming to help him than Genevieve Drake. "I know it's a lot to ask. But because of the information's sensitivity, my options are sorely limited."

"You talked to your dad about this?"

It was a fair question. Donovan talked to his dad about everything. "No." Almost. "I thought there was no need to ask Dad without asking you first."

"Really?"

Yeah, I don't believe it either.

"Because had you done so, you'd know that your father and I are handling some family business this week."

"What kind of family business?" Nothing happened with one Drake that the others didn't know about.

"With all of the activity surrounding your sister's wedding, we hadn't had time to tell you about this. But we're finally going to divide up that property on my mother's side. You know it's going to be crazy with everybody trying to get their piece of the pie. I'd just as soon deed my part to whoever wants it just to keep the peace. But not my sister. She's determined that some cousins, who weren't on speaking terms with their great-aunt's brother, won't get so much as a teaspoon of dirt! She wants me to come down to support her."

Donovan sat back and rubbed his brow. The timing of this situation sucked.

"Donovan, even if this trip weren't planned, I'd be like a fish out of water in the office. Not to mention navigating the dynamic of your being my boss."

"I'd go easy on you."

"You'd have a choice?"

"Ha! Guess not."

Donovan knew he was out of all options except one. And with that he picked up his cell and made a call.

"Hello."

"Marissa, this is Donovan." *Okay, man. Here we go.*

Chapter 7

She almost asked, "Donovan who?" Such was her surprise. But in Marissa's world, there was only one. The one she'd been thinking of almost incessantly since yesterday. The one whose voice was the last one she'd imagined hearing today.

"Hello." And again, the type of silence between them that begged for a word...or a cricket chirp.

"Yes, Marissa, do you have a minute?"

I'm about to have a heart attack, but that wasn't your question. She cleared her throat. "Yes. I'm glad you called, Donovan," she said, determined to straighten her big-girl backbone and act like she'd known how to converse since the age of two. "I wanted to apologize for snapping at you after the rehearsal dinner. Diamond told me that your assistant, Sharon, had to have surgery, and I'm sure the news was stressful to you. I hope she'll be doing better soon."

"Your apology is accepted, and I hope you'll accept mine, as well. Stress is never a reason to be rude. I'm sorry for snapping back."

"So how is she?"

"Doing better, thanks." Marissa waited for further comment. She'd said what she wanted to say; now it was up to Donovan to say why he'd called. "Jackson gave me your number before he left."

"Oh."

"It's work related," Donovan quickly clarified.

"Oh."

Amazing how the same word could be said in two totally different ways.

Marissa heard Donovan chuckle, and the sound sent an unexpected shiver down her spine. Instantly, she realized two things. One, she hadn't heard Donovan laugh before, and two, she really liked how it sounded: warm and deep, like the still waters she felt flowed beneath that professional, businesslike exterior he showed to the world.

"That probably came out wrong. I just didn't want you to get the impression that I was trying to hit on you."

"Okay," Marissa said, drawing out the word.

"This hole just keeps getting deeper, doesn't it?"

"You are kinda giving a shovel some competition."

"Then I'll get to the point. Jackson said that the administrative workload at Boss Construction would be fairly light these next two weeks, and he volunteered you for a project I'm working on."

"I thought the mice were supposed to play when the boss was away."

"That's usually the way it works. Perhaps when he

gets back I can talk him into giving you an extra week's vacation as compensation…along with the money you'll be paid for your work here."

"So I'm going to continue receiving my salary through Boss Construction and *you're* going to pay me?"

"That's right."

"Well, Donovan, that's a hard offer to refuse." Believing that Donovan was waiting for her answer, she asked him, "When do I start?"

"Bright and early tomorrow morning, let's say nine o'clock. Also, you live in San Diego, correct?"

"Right."

"I live in La Jolla, but because of the intensity of these next two weeks, I'm staying at the resort. Would it be a problem for you to stay here, as well? We'll be keeping late hours, and staying here will alleviate the time you'd spend in rush hour traffic."

For many reasons, including a man whose unexpected reappearance in her life had left her paranoid and whose motives were still unclear, she didn't hesitate. "No, Donovan, that wouldn't be a problem at all. You said for two weeks, correct?"

"Yes."

"Does that include the weekend?"

"I'm sorry, Marissa, but probably yes. We'll more than likely be working around the clock."

"That's fine, I just wanted to know how much to pack."

"Any other questions?"

"No. I guess I'll learn everything about the project tomorrow."

"That you will. I'll see you then."

"Okay, Donovan. I'll see you tomorrow morning."

Marissa ended the call and felt a flutter of nervousness in her stomach. She knew that her uneasiness had nothing to do with whether or not she could handle the assignment and everything to do with whether or not she could handle the man.

The following morning, a bright and sunny Monday without a cloud in the sky, a fairly confident Marissa arrived at Drake Wines Resort and Spa. She entered the lobby and followed the gold-plated signs past the still-closed gift shop, up a flight of stairs to the second floor and down a hallway to a set of double doors. Hesitating for just a second, just long enough to take a calming breath, she opened the door, stepped inside and walked up to the young woman seated behind a low-slung counter.

"Hello. May I help you?"

"Yes, Marissa Hayes to see Donovan Drake."

The perky receptionist with the warm, sincere smile touched a button on her switchboard. After announcing that Marissa had arrived, she asked if Marissa wanted a morning beverage. After Marissa declined, the receptionist directed her to a seat in a cozily designed waiting area just across from the receptionist counter. Instead of sitting, Marissa took the time to admire the brightly colored artwork, the bronze table whatnots and the live jade plant.

"Ms. Hayes?" Marissa turned to see another smiling, welcoming face. As she followed this assistant back through a beautifully appointed space—silk-covered, beige-colored walls, deep-ply tan carpeting, burnished mahogany and accessories in various metals—she was struck by the irony of life, how not so long ago her world seemed bleak and almost unbearable. Her parents' relocation, a friend's betrayal and leaving a job she loved as a result of that betrayal had sent Marissa's world into turmoil where she questioned all and trusted none. Then she'd met Jackson Wright and got the job with Boss Construction. The work, her fellow employees and her trustworthy boss became her anchors, and she was content to build her world around them. She hadn't thought about dating or bringing a significant other into her life. So why was she thinking about it now?

The answer was just around the corner, talking on the phone as he waved her in. The assistant who'd brought her to Donovan's office gave a brief nod and closed the door on her way out. Marissa forced herself to meet Donovan's eyes, hooded brown treasures that seemed to drink her in as she walked to one of two chocolate-colored leather chairs in front of his massive oak desk. She sat down, placed her hands in her lap, feigned a deep interest in the trappings of Donovan's office and resigned herself to the fact that these were going to be the longest two weeks of her life.

Chapter 8

"I look forward to meeting with you. Ha! Yes, I'll pack my golf clubs. You're past due for a whipping on the green. All right then, goodbye." Donovan stood as he placed the phone back on the cradle. "Good morning," he said with his hand outstretched, his tone clipped and businesslike.

"Good morning." Marissa stood and clasped his hand.

And there was that jolt of electricity again.

"Ooh! I must have…rubbed my heel against the carpet."

Donovan quickly removed his hand and walked back behind his desk. He was not at all happy at his body's reaction to seeing Marissa this morning, or at her audacity to look so delicious. *This is work; not a fashion show!* "I see there's one thing I forgot to mention," he said as they both retook their seats. "Initially, you'll be spending a lot of time retrieving information from stored boxes and then schlepping those files containing the information here to be inputted into our database. Did you pack anything more casual?" *Plain, dowdy, loose-fitting, something that doesn't hug your curves like a sports car?*

Marissa looked down at her dress as though she'd forgotten what she was wearing. It had taken her more than an hour to decide on what she thought was a simple yet becoming navy dress and three-inch pumps; she'd felt they looked appropriately serious with her hair pulled back in a plain ponytail, with a couple tendrils kept loose near the sides of her head and the nape of her neck. "I packed a couple pairs of jeans for after hours," she responded. "And flats for when I wasn't on the job."

"This morning, I'll give you an overview of what will be happening during your time here, show you around the office, let you see where you'll be working. After lunch, you'll want to change into something more comfortable—" immediately Donovan's mind went somewhere it shouldn't "—into something that you won't mind getting dirty."

"Of course."

"Okay." Donovan paused, wishing he could think of some other reason to chide her. As long as he was putting her in her place, he figured he could forget about putting her in his bed; the singular thought that had occupied his conscience since they'd last met. "Why don't we start by introducing you around."

For the next half an hour, Marissa met those in the sales area where she'd be doing some of her work and was also shown the break room, bathroom, lounge and gym. After that, Donovan left her—translated, dumped her off—with Diamond's assistant, Kathleen Fitzpatrick, who had graciously delayed her vacation by one day to familiarize Marissa with the system used companywide. Tomorrow, a representative from the new program that had been installed would walk her through how to transfer the data. After her working lunch, where Kathleen continued to show Marissa the straightforward yet multilayered program, Marissa changed from dress to jeans, and she spent the afternoon in the storage room amid thousands of files recently received from Asia. That's where Donovan found her around six o'clock.

Or rather her booty, because that's what his eyes zoomed in on as he rounded the corner, pushed against the pulled-to-but-not-shut door in the files room and saw her. She'd emptied a box and had set up some type of system on the floor by which she was organizing the papers inside. At the time, he'd thought it a good idea to get her out of that mouthwatering navy number, to suggest she lose her heels and choose something more suited for the task at hand. But he didn't know that she'd look as sexy in a pair of black jeans, a printed cotton top and a pair of wedge-style black sandals as she did in the dress. He watched her and noted how when concentrating her brow furrowed slightly and she nibbled on her lip in a way that he'd like to. He felt himself getting warm and growing hard, and his admiration quickly turned to irritation. He didn't have time to be ogling the help. He wasn't at all interested in pursuing a relationship and, since her boss was his brother-in-law, didn't think he'd score so well with a one-night stand. No, he had to stay in firm and absolute control of this situation; be the boss in every way possible. *Yes, that's right. You're the boss. You're the one in control here.* If he repeated this mantra long enough, maybe it would come true.

"That's enough for today," he said, his voice coming out harder than he intended.

Marissa jumped. "Oh! I didn't hear you walk up." She got up from her crouched position and smoothed an errant strand of curly black hair that had escaped the clasp. "I know it looks like a mess now, but there's a method to my madness."

"I'm sure there is, and first thing tomorrow morning will be time enough to get back at it. We don't want to overwork you."

"Oh, it's no trouble at all. Actually, I'm one of those rare ones who actually likes to organize, make sense out of mayhem. I'm almost done with this box and would like to finish it before I leave. No more than half an hour and I'll be out."

Donovan continued to stand there, wrestling with his edict to stay in control and with how juvenile it would seem to demand that she leave, that she not finish a project. How stupid would that sound? "I think tomorrow will be soon enough to finish the task."

Marissa looked at Donovan a long moment before delivering a short, clipped "okay." She reached for her purse on top of a file cabinet and walked past him—head high and booty swaying—down the hall and around the corner.

Damn! Why'd you do that? Why can't you keep it together with that chick? Donovan walked into Marissa's temporary world. He looked around at the neat stacks, some topped with sticky notes designating what needed to go where, along with the information to be inputted and in what order. Her handwriting was smooth and deliberate, like her, with no extraneous curlicues or stars for dots. Upon closing his eyes, he realized he could still smell her perfume, something fruity yet floral. Eyes still closed, he saw that look she'd given him before hurriedly exiting the room. What was that in her eyes? Anger? Chagrin, surely. But…there was something else. Leaving the room and closing the door behind him, Donovan figured it was anyone's guess what was on the mind of Marissa Hayes. His mind though? Simple. Her. If Donovan was going to survive the next two weeks, he was going to have to do something about it.

Nothing like a family dinner to get your mind on other things. At least this was Donovan's thought as he entered the sprawling main house that made up the Drake estate. In addition to the home where his grand-parents lived, there were also two guesthouses, a pool house and stables on the other side of their private pond. He was more than happy with his La Jolla spread and the privacy it afforded, but there were times when he missed the camaraderie that came with the entire Drake clan living under one roof.

"Dang, man. What's wrong with you?"

Missing the nosiness? Not so much. "Who said any-thing's wrong?" Donovan passed Dexter and entered a cozy room off of the den that was mostly used to pass time, sip wine and discuss whatever. There was a bottle of one of the vineyard's exclusive wines, PNDO—Pinot Noir Drake Original—resting on the counter. "This was left over from the wedding?"

Dexter nodded. "We have five bottles that can now be imbibed at will."

"Make sure they don't all end up in your wing."

"My product, my prerogative." Dexter walked over to the counter and poured two glasses of the deep maroon-colored liquid. He gave one of the large wineglasses to Donovan. "So," Dexter said, having chosen not to use the aerator in favor of slowly swirling the wine, "was that Jackson's assistant I saw walking from the offices to the hotel suites?" Donovan nodded. "What's she doing here?"

"She's helping me with the Asian database project."

"So what has you in this sour mood?" Dexter asked, his eyes twinkling because he thought he already knew the answer. "The ramp-up or the fine *rump* on that sister helping you get the work done?"

"Marissa's attractive, but it's not her looks I'm interested in, it's her skill set."

"Hmm. Then I guess she's not too happy about that."

Donovan took a drink, tried to act nonchalant. "How you figure?"

"Because I saw her leaving the office. She too had quite the scowl on her face. If I didn't know you better, I'd say it was a lover's quarrel."

"But you do know me better. And you know that sleeping with every skirt that passes is your thing."

"Then what happened?"

"She wanted to keep working," Donovan said with a shrug. "I told her to call it a day."

Dexter's wineglass stopped in midair. "What? Mr. Workaholic himself told someone else to clock out?" Dexter walked over to one of two tufted leather chairs and took a seat. "She must be really getting to you. Got you so out of sorts that at a time when we're trying to pack forty-eight hours of work into twenty-four-hour days, you're forcing someone to knock off early. I can understand though. The sister's beautiful—nice face, tight body. Who knows. I might even—"

"Don't even go there, Dex."

"What? If you're not interested then why can't I sample the goods? You say she's going to be here for how long?"

"For the time that our sister and her boss are on their honeymoon."

"Oh, right. Her working with Boss could be a complication. You know, for when I get tired of her and all and she begs me not to leave her." Dexter shrugged. Donovan scowled. "But she's grown. Anything the two of us did would have to be by mutual consent, believe that."

"Stay away from her, Dex. She doesn't need somebody like you messing with her head."

"One, how do you know what she needs? And two, what makes you think that her head is what I want to mess with?"

In an uncharacteristic show of anger, Donovan was in Dexter's face in two seconds flat. "Leave her alone," he growled, his finger in a calm and somewhat bemused Dexter's face. "I mean it. She is off-limits. Don't make me—"

"I thought I—" Genevieve rounded the corner and stopped short. The brothers tried to act casual—Dexter slowly sipping his wine, Donovan looking out the window, his hands stuffed in his pockets—but the tension in the room could be cut with a Samurai sword... maybe. Genevieve didn't seem fazed. "Who stole whose marbles?" she dryly asked, a question she'd often posed to the men when they were boys.

Dexter walked over to his mom and enveloped her in a bear hug.

"Get off me, boy!" Genevieve's laughter belied the gruffness of her tone. "Trying to divert my attention. I heard y'all arguing."

"Naw, just schooling your son on the world of women—"

"What's for dinner?" Donovan's desire to change the subject was about as subtle as a preacher in a playboy club. He went to Genevieve's other side and the two men walked with their mother toward the dining room.

"Smells like roast," Genevieve said in a serious tone. "But sounds like chicken. You boys finish up whatever you were *discussing*. Dinner is in five minutes."

"Whoa, man," Dexter said after making sure their mother was no longer in the hall. "I was messing with you, just jerking your chain. Calm down!" He watched Donovan finish a half a glass of wine in one swallow. "I'm sorry, man. You're really feeling her, aren't you?"

"I shouldn't be. Situation's dicey, timing's all wrong."

"What's the situation?"

"Not sure," Donovan said, shaking his head. "But it has something to do with a former male friend who she swears is not an ex but who has her skittish about getting involved with anyone. Of course, that could be her excuse for not getting involved with me, but that's what she told me. Then there's the matter of her working for Boss. If we started dating and then broke up that could be uncomfortable."

"I wouldn't worry about that, man. We've got to live each day to the fullest and let the chips fall where they may. I say you should go after her. She'll be here what, two weeks?"

Donovan did a mental calculation. "As of tomorrow, because the Fourth falls on a Friday, nine days."

"Then I'd say you've got nine days to get in those panties."

"Dexter…"

"I'm just saying, brother. That's a whole bunch of badonkadonk right there. Shame to let all that go to waste."

"There you go again, man."

"What? I'm just saying."

"Well quit saying. And quit looking, too. Marissa Hayes is off-limits. You got it?"

Dexter nodded. "Got it."

"Good. Let's go eat."

Chapter 9

Two hours of shopping and a whole medium pizza later, Marissa was slightly less angry than she'd been three hours ago. Just who did Donovan Drake think he was to order her off the job like a ten-year-old? When Marissa Hayes started a job, she finished it or at least she left it at a sensible point for her to begin the next day. After an afternoon of familiarizing herself with the file's contents and their office's system and then finally creating a structure that would work for expedient input of the material into a database, she'd just hit her stride and had actually begun enjoying her work. So much so that there had been a smile on her face and a song in her heart at just around six o'clock, just around the time she'd looked around, figured another hour or so would set her up perfectly for the following day. And then he had to come through, with his scowl and Donovan Downer personality and mess up her day. *Ugh!*

By the time Marissa's phone rang, she'd become angry all over again. "Hey, Mom."

"Oh, goodness." Yolanda Hayes's perpetually calm voice flowed through the phone and brought a bit of peace to the storm. "Someone's unhappy."

Marissa rolled her eyes. *You think?* Yolanda Hayes was truly a wonderful woman whom Marissa loved very much. As mother-daughter relationships went, theirs was a close one. But in Marissa's twenty-nine years on the planet, she could count her mother's bad days on one hand. To her knowledge, there had been three: when she found out about the scandal involving her husband's minister-friend; when she put Nippy, the family's beloved thirteen-year-old cocker spaniel, to sleep; and the day that Marissa's grandfather had died and joined his wife in the hereafter. In Marissa's eyes, her mother had always been this perfect soul, the epitome of womanhood, the type of person that Marissa could never live up to. It didn't matter that Yolanda was not perfect and would never expect her daughter to be; it was the fact that in Marissa's mind Yolanda Hayes was flawless and would be devastated to learn about some of Marissa's past actions. For these reasons, Marissa tried to swallow her anger and put some sugar in her voice.

"Sorry, Mom. It was a long today. I'm a bit tired, I guess."

"Isn't your boss on his honeymoon?"

"Yes, and while he's away, I'm working on a special assignment with his wife's brother."

"Marissa Lynn, if this work is making you unhappy, perhaps you should just walk away."

That the work was fine and the boss was the problem was a fact Marissa chose not to divulge. "I'll be fine,

Mom. A good night's sleep will work wonders. Speaking of, isn't it a little late for you to call?"

"I just finished talking to your brother, Timothy. He and Nicole are expecting another baby!"

"That's great, Mom." Great. Really. Just what she needed. Again, she loved her brother and would get around to being genuinely happy about his news. But tonight it was a reminder of milestones she had not reached—marriage and motherhood.

"Your father and I are ecstatic at having a second grandchild. There's only one thing that would make me happier."

Uh-oh. That's my cue. "Look, Mom. Hate to cut you off but I'm back at the resort and need to unload my trunk."

"Resort? Why are you staying at a resort?"

Just what she hadn't meant to do; make her mother even more curious about her life than she was already. "Remember I told you that Jackson's wife's family owns a resort? That's where I'm working. To save time in driving back and forth, I'm staying here while working on the project."

"That sounds wonderful, baby! So tell me this. Is this brother you're working with married and, if not, is he a prospect? You're not getting any younger, Marissa, and while I'd always hoped that your and Steven's relationship would have blossomed into something romantic, you need to think of your future."

Marissa wheeled her car into a parking space. "I'll call you this weekend, Mom." She ended the call. By the time she entered her room with multiple shopping bags in tow, a smoldering sadness had replaced the previous anger brought on by Donovan's actions and an unexplainable weariness had seeped into her pores. While hanging up the purchases that a short time ago had brought joy, two major questions plagued her: *How did I get here and where am I going?*

The first question was the easiest. After graduating college and armed with a bachelor's in business administration, Marissa had been more than happy to take up Steven's offer and get a job at the large technology firm where he was employed. This time in her life had been great: getting promoted to junior management, becoming engaged to the man she thought would become her husband and Steven continuing to be her best bud. But then, in the blink of an eye, her life unraveled. She found out her boyfriend turned/fiancé that she'd dated for four years had one child who was three and another who'd just turned two (bad math in anybody's relationship classroom). Her best friend betrayed her and, as a result, she had to leave the job she loved. Enter Jackson Wright, who needed an assistant when she desperately needed a job. She didn't think twice about taking what most would consider a demotion, feeling instantly at home and protected at Boss Construction, surrounded by rugged men who quickly became loyal friends. Without providing details, Jackson had perceived Marissa's vulnerability. After working there awhile, Jackson gained her trust, and she confided to him what Steven had done. After that, she was sure he'd warned his guys off of her because in all the time she'd worked for him, the men had treated her with nothing but respect. Her gratitude was evident in the tireless way she worked, throwing herself lock, stock and barrel into becoming the best executive assistant on the planet; she was thankful for the diversion that served to keep the bad thoughts at bay. Except on nights like tonight when she was fully aware of the facts: she was twenty-nine and counting, unwed with no prospects while many of her college associates were on marriage number two and baby number three.

It was also on nights like these that she wished she'd worked harder on making friends during her high school and college years. But she'd always been a bit of a loner. On her first day at college she'd met Steven, the gregarious, rambunctious ball of energy who was the night to her day, who'd been all the friend she'd needed to navigate the next several years. On that first day of their friendship's beginning, she could never have imagined how it would end. Marissa shook her head to bring her out of those unfortunate musings.

There was the matter of the second question: Where was she going? As Marissa climbed into bed the only thing she knew for sure was that the foreseeable future—at least the next several days—were going to be spent at Drake Wines Resort and Spa working alongside Donovan Drake. Considering what she'd been through and the drama she'd navigated, surely she could handle him. She went to sleep determined to find the high road with this temporary assignment, take it and then run back to her safe haven at Boss Construction, where hard work was valued and the workday wasn't sandwiched between nine and five. That's what she thought as she went to sleep, but in her dreams, once again, her cavorting with Donovan had nothing to do with the workplace and everything to do with the bedroom.

Chapter 10

"Good morning!" Marissa's voice rivaled that of a bluebird announcing the dawning of a new day. She'd gotten up bright and early, exulted in a long, hot shower, curled her hair, dressed in her new casually fun sundress and flat sandals and eaten a scrumptious breakfast akin to that of a boxer the day of a fight. Though she'd tossed and turned much of the night, she was no less determined to put her best foot forward and have a great day. Even if it killed her.

Donovan stood at the entrance to the storage room, taking in her attire. *Good morning? Says who?* "I thought we'd agreed to dress casual?"

This from a man who stood in tailored black slacks, a starched tan shirt, striped tie and—if Marissa were not mistaken—a recently groomed goatee?

"This is casual," she replied. "Besides, my mother always said that looking good is feeling good. How are you feeling today?" *Because you're looking as tasty as this morning's French toast.*

With almost no sleep and his waking hours filled with thoughts of the vixen in front of him, he was feeling about as cheerful as a grizzly. But he figured there was no need to show his hand. "I'm good," he said with a curt nod. And then with barely a breath he continued, "We've got a lot to do today. Meet me in my office in half an hour and we'll get you started on today's input."

"But what about these files?"

"They can wait. A half hour. Don't be late."

It wasn't until she'd slammed down the fifth manila folder onto the pile, sending the folders beneath it scattering in different directions, that Marissa realized that once again, Donovan was sticking in her proverbial craw. "It's ridiculous," she muttered, kneeling down to pick up the strewn papers and errant sticky posts. Absolutely insane. The fact that she'd ever thought the man who was now her merciless tormentor was either attractive or intelligent was impossible to believe. Even now she was as angry with herself as with him for the fact that her heart had quickened in his very presence and that it may have even skipped a beat. And then he'd opened his mouth. "You try and do a great job, try and be nice, and what do you get? Total ungratefulness," she hissed through clenched teeth. "And about as much personality as a resident of the wax museum."

"Good morning!"

Marissa inwardly grimaced at the sound in the doorway, and prayed that her mumbling hadn't been overheard. "Good morning, Dexter." She turned to greet him before hurrying back to her task.

"You know what they say," Dexter continued casually as he strolled into the room. "People who talk to themselves either wish to converse with a highly intelligent audience...or have a screw loose."

"Ha!" Marissa relaxed even as she noted how different the two brothers were. Where Donovan was reserved, Dexter was flamboyant and devil-may-care. Where Donovan seemed to take every moment of life seriously, Dexter seemed to tease fate, living each moment as if it were his last. And while Marissa appreciated his endless party lifestyle, she also knew that dating such an individual would drive her crazy. "I'm probably guilty of a little of both."

"I thought I saw you last night. And then Donovan told me that you were helping him with our international expansion into the Asian market."

The frown jumped on her face before she could stop it. "Yes, well..."

"A little trouble in paradise or, in this case, the vineyard?" When Marissa didn't answer, Dexter walked to the door and pushed it closed. "We're practically family, Marissa. You can talk to me."

Marissa sighed as she leaned against the large filing cabinet. A part of her wanted no part of voicing her thoughts out loud; the other part relished a second opinion. "I'm not quite sure whether your brother and I are very different or too much alike. Either way, we sort of got off on the wrong foot." Marissa told Dexter about the night of the engagement party and how she'd not met Donovan as they'd initially planned. She left out the part about Steven's participation, hidden behind the more general "something came up."

Dexter listened intently, arms crossed, pose casual as he leaned against the wall. "Let me tell you something about my brother," he said once she'd finished. "He's the serious one of the siblings, a 'strictly business' kind of guy. But he's a good man, too, who can be very focused when it comes to something he wants or cares about."

"Look, I know how important this project is to him and to your company. He's made me very aware of how confidential it is, how critical it is to this next phase in your business plan, all of that. I understand that, and I've told him that while I know I can't take Sharon's place, I will do my very best to pick up the slack in her absence."

"I have no doubt that you will," Dexter said, raising off the wall and heading toward the door. "But when it comes to what Donovan wants, I'm not talking about a job well done. I'm talking about you."

"What?" Marissa sprang forward from leaning against the file cabinet, her back becoming ramrod straight.

Dexter chuckled. "You heard me. My brother is digging you. And from your reaction, I'd say the feeling is mutual."

By the time Marissa got her mouth working, Dexter's whistle could be heard down the hall.

Chapter 11

Thank goodness for Chad Witter, owner of Data Design and Solutions. He was the angel Marissa found seated in Donovan's office when she arrived there a full five minutes before his be-there-in-half-an-hour-don't-be-late command. At least she wouldn't have to be alone with Donovan.

Dexter's parting comments had left her reeling, and wondering. Was Dexter speculating when it came to his brother's feelings about her? And why had he assumed she had feelings for Donovan when she hadn't even acknowledged those feelings to herself? All of these questions and speculations she hid behind a shield of complete professionalism: asking the right questions, nodding in the appropriate places. But what was really on her mind was Dexter's comment: *he's digging you.* That and images from her dream last night—she and

Donovan together, quite alone and quite naked, on the hilltop in the moonlight. Their bodies, sweaty, entwined in the throes of passion. His tongue searching, capturing, devouring. His lips, those lips, those lips moving and talking and...

"Marissa?"

"Oh, sorry, Donovan. I was pondering what Chad just said."

A quick look passed between Chad and Donovan. "It normally doesn't take much thought to answer where one graduated college," Donovan said, his voice laced with humor. "Although understandable that some of us want to forget about those campus days."

Busted. But Marissa put her 3.8 GPA to use and recovered in a bat of an eyelash. "Forgive me. I'm still thinking about the translation and formatting component to this software, Chad, and ways that by tweaking the columns, this could possibly be used in the categorizing of wines, as well, specifically the new inventory against the present selections, and the exclusive ones developed for the wine bars. It would streamline the entire inventory process, cataloguing by type, year, whatever details are important. I'm sorry," she said when she realized she was going on and on. She switched her attention from Chad to Donovan. "I know my work here is limited primarily to the customer base, but in my mind, it's an obvious parallel."

"No apology needed," Donovan replied, a flicker of new awareness and admiration in his eyes as he slowly stroked his goatee. From the moment he'd met Marissa she'd seemed to be a study in contradictions. Sort of like an onion, with layer after layer to peel away. But if there was any place that he was certain they could have a fairly innocuous meeting of the minds, it was around business. This was, after all, the only reason she was here, right? Donovan determined at that moment that he wanted to peel back the various veneers to the mystery woman seated near him. And he wanted to start tonight.

After another hour, the meeting with Chad wrapped up. "Thanks for everything," Donovan said as he stood, signaling the end of the discussion. Marissa stood, as well.

"No problem, buddy," Chad replied, putting his mini-computer and papers into his briefcase and then joining Marissa and Donovan near the center of the office. "I'm just happy to see our product do what it is supposed to do and that is make our customers' lives easier and their work more streamlined." He turned to Marissa. "It was my pleasure to meet you," he continued, his hand out-stretched. "If there is anything that you need, anything at all, please don't hesitate to contact our office." He held her hand in his, his blue eyes sparkling with open admiration. Marissa smiled back, genuinely impressed with the products Chad and his company had developed.

But somebody wasn't a fan of this mutual admiration society. "Yes," Donovan said, his voice authoritative as he reached out his hand. "I'll call you if we need anything. Good seeing you again, Chad."

Marissa's brow rose ever so slightly. *Can we say dismissed?*

"Marissa," Donovan said to her retreating back as she started to follow Chad out.

She stopped in the doorway, and the way the sun from the window framed her face it was as though she wore a halo.

Angel or devil, Ms. Hayes, Donovan thought. *Which*

are you? "I appreciated your input just now. It was obvious that we hit upon your niche."

"At one time I thought about getting my degree in computer programming," she admitted. "But at the end of my sophomore year Ste—uh, a friend convinced me that a degree in business administration would be more versatile."

"I see. So armed with your degree and obvious intelligence, why are you a secretary?"

Marissa wasn't offended by the question, although, on the part of working assistants everywhere, she could have been. But she more than understood. It was one her parents had repeatedly asked when she left—translated, fled—the job where she'd held a junior management position. "Timing. Jackson needed an assistant. I needed a job. I'm very happy working with Boss."

The astute brain that made Donovan an excellent businessman immediately sensed more to the story. "He's a good man. But that still doesn't explain why you're in a position that some would consider beneath your education and skill set."

Marissa looked beyond Donovan's shoulder and took in the picture-perfect day as she pondered his question. "It's a long story," she finally said.

"Well, I'd like to hear it if you don't mind," Donovan easily countered. "Over dinner, tonight, seven o'clock."

"It's not something that I feel comfortable sharing," Marissa said. "So thanks for the dinner invite, but I think I'll just do room service."

"I'm sorry if that sounded like a question," Donovan said, his mannerism all business as he walked to his desk, sat and began shuffling papers. "What you choose to share with me is your option. Dinner is not. I'll meet you at Grapevine at seven." Ignoring her frown, he continued, "Right now, I need help with some handouts for an important meeting tomorrow. I have a lot of information to cover, but I'd like to have it organized succinctly in no more than a one- to two-page handout. Do you think you can handle something like that?"

Marissa crossed her arms and hid a smirk. "I believe I can."

"Good." He went through the papers on his desk, pulled out various facts and figures and told her the results he hoped to achieve. "Any questions?"

"No, it sounds pretty straightforward. I'll draft a couple different layouts and have you approve the one that suits your needs before proceeding."

"Perfect. That's it for now. Remember dinner, tonight, Grapevine, seven sharp." He looked up from the papers in an authoritative manner that Marissa found quite annoying. "Don't be late."

Donovan hit a computer key and began scrolling through his calendar for the rest of the day's activities, a clear (if rude) indicator that their meeting and conversation was over. Marissa stood there for several long seconds, debating on what if anything she should say in parting. Finally, because she couldn't resist saying something, she pulled up her utmost Southern drawl and replied, "Yessah, massa." Then, still in a huff, she turned on her heel and walked out.

Donovan continued scrolling through his calendar, but a wisp of a smile turned his lips up a little bit.

That evening, Marissa arrived at the vineyard's premiere restaurant shortly before seven. In characteristically passive-aggressive fashion, she'd ignored

Donovan's suggestion for casualness in the workplace and donned the one suit she'd packed. It was her favorite: a very professional yet form-enhancing St. John number. The one-button jacket accented her plentiful breasts and small waist while the skirt stopped a few inches from the knee, showing off legs surprisingly long for someone of her stature. She paired the perfectly cut yet simple black suit with an equally understated white shell with thin black stripes, simple silver jewelry and minimal makeup. Her hair was in a loose chignon, wisps of curls framing her face and caressing her neck. Spiky black pumps and a splash of perfume completed the look. If she couldn't feel good, which was becoming an increasing possibility where being around Donovan was concerned, then she was going to look good.

She walked to the restaurant's entrance and stood near the hostess station. Thinking of his love of wine, she glanced toward the bar but didn't see him.

"Hello," said the hostess, who'd just returned to her station. "Will someone be joining you this evening?"

"Yes," Marissa replied still looking around. "They'll be one more."

"May I have your name?"

"Marissa Hayes."

"Ah, Ms. Hayes. Mr. Drake is already here. If you'll follow me, please."

Marissa followed the hostess farther into the restaurant. For a week night it was fairly crowded and Marissa was glad she didn't have to search out Donovan on her own. They continued through the main dining area and around a corner. *Can we be any farther in the back? Because of my parting statement, did he think I'd show up with a kerchief on my head?* Before Marissa's indignation could get any more righteous, they turned yet another corner and crossed the hall to another door. After a slight tap, the hostess opened the door to a private dining room, smaller than the one where Diamond's rehearsal dinner had been held, yet equal in its tasteful appointment. "Mr. Drake, your guest," she said before stepping back to let Marissa enter. Donovan stood and thanked the hostess, almost stopping Marissa in her tracks. He too had dressed for whatever occasion was about to happen and looked perfectly dapper in a chocolate-brown suit, a black shirt open at the collar and those deep chocolate orbs relentlessly trained on her.

It was going to be an interesting evening.

Chapter 12

Entering the private dining room Marissa became coy, almost shy. "You're looking quite—" *what was the word?* "—dapper, Mr. Drake," she said, as he pulled out her chair to be seated. "What's the occasion?"

Donovan sat back down, stroked his goatee. "I was just about to ask you the same question."

"A chance to wear one of the dressier outfits I packed," she said with a shrug. She took a sip of her water, looked around the room. "What about you? Special night?" Marissa giggled, part nervousness, part flirt. The evening was not at all turning out as she'd envisioned, something that with Donovan Drake was becoming routine.

"I don't know why I chose to dress up," Donovan said truthfully. "But I'm glad I did." He nodded toward an open bottle of bubbly chilling in a silver bucket. "Would you like a drink?"

"I guess one glass in the middle of the week will be okay."

Donovan arched a brow. "Only one?"

"Wouldn't want to get hungover," Marissa countered. "My boss is a slave driver."

"Ha!" His countenance turned serious. "Marissa, you and I seem to have gotten off on the wrong foot. I want to change that."

Nodding slowly, Marissa answered, "Me, too."

From seemingly out of nowhere two waiters appeared. One placed down two salad plates while the other set down a basket of rolls and topped off their lemon waters. The first then poured two flutes of champagne and, after an almost imperceptive nod from Donovan, soundlessly retreated through a side door.

Donovan didn't reach for the bubbly right away. Instead he looked at Marissa, his intense and thoughtful gaze causing her heartbeat to quicken and her thighs to clench. "I want to apologize for my sometimes boorish behavior," he said at last. "I take the business quite seriously and when I'm focused, I know I can be a bit short. I'm sorry."

Marissa smiled. Donovan held his breath and captured what was for him an angelic image on the camera in his mind. "Thank you, Donovan. I too apologize for…everything."

Donovan was tempted to bring it up again, that night so many months ago that started the conflict. He still wondered about the man at the bar, the one Marissa said she knew. The reason that she didn't come in. Who was he? An ex-boyfriend most likely, though she'd denied it. But why else would it matter to the guy who Marissa dated? The thought of her being with someone else didn't sit well with Donovan at all. He didn't like imagining another man enjoying her subdued charm, didn't like picturing anyone's hands on her but his. And following these thoughts, Dexter's words floated to the fore. *We've got to live each day to the fullest and let the chips fall where they may. I say you should go after her.* Dexter was absolutely right. Life was short, and this window of uninterrupted opportunity was shorter. Eight days, now. That's how long he had to wear down the armor Marissa had seemingly built up around her heart. Whatever had happened in her past, Donovan knew he had his work cut out for him.

He reached for the champagne flute and lifted the glass. "To new beginnings."

Marissa followed suit. "To new beginnings and great working relationships."

"Hear, hear."

They drank, and the sparkle in Marissa's eyes rivaled that in the glass of fruity ambrosia with a hint of a kick.

"I'm not much of a champagne drinker, but this is really nice," she said after a couple sips.

Donovan nodded. "It's still a work in progress, part of the exclusive line that we're developing for the Asian market and a few other select clientele. This top-shelf product will only be available in the most exclusive of establishments. It's been aging for five years and will be uncorked and publicly unveiled for the first time during the holidays. That's what this is…one of our latest creations."

"What is it called?"

"We don't know yet. Dexter's department has been tossing several names around. Boss suggested that we call it Diamond."

"I like that!"

"So does his wife," was Donovan's dry reply.

"I can see calling it Diamond rather than Dexter or Donovan."

"Ha! You have a point."

Marissa smiled and took a sip of the champagne before placing the flute on the table. The champagne was not only delicious, but potent. She could already feel a buzz. "So, Dexter is the winemaker?"

"Among other things. Our parents raised us to know all aspects of the business and juggle multiple responsibilities. Along with being the head winemaker, he's also director of Business Development. I'm CFO, but also spend quite a bit of time in sales, my initial position after graduate school. Thus, my heading up the international expansion, working very closely with my dad."

"And Diamond is the director of PR and Marketing, right?"

"Right. But as you know she also headed up the last phase of our renovation."

"And did an excellent job," Marissa said, again looking around the room. "And while doing so she met Boss, and the rest is history."

"At least that part of it," Donovan agreed, taking another sip of his drink. "But considering tonight, I'd say that history is still being made."

"How so?"

Donovan shrugged. "I guess we'll see." He motioned to Marissa's plate. "After you."

"Of course." Marissa placed the stark white linen napkin in her lap and took a bite of the salad filled with herbs and greens from the vineyard's large, organic garden.

"How's your room?"

"Absolutely gorgeous! I love how all of the rooms are themed by colors and wines."

"Which one are you in?" Donovan took a generous bite of salad and reached for one of the freshly baked rolls still warm and waiting beneath a heavy napkin.

"The Chardonnay Suite, which, again, is very generous of you. Considering the hours I'll be working, a regular room would have been more than enough."

"We wanted to take care of you."

"The layers of cream and champagne paired with the platinum fixtures and accessories give the room a very rich yet light feel."

"You'll have to let Diamond know how much you like it. She'll appreciate it."

"You guys seem like a really close-knit family."

"We are."

"I read a little about the history of Drake Wines. But what about your family history? Do you mind sharing?"

"Not at all." His countenance became as relaxed as Marissa had seen it as he chatted easily, initially forgoing her question about the family to describe the evening's wines. Waiters returned and removed their salad plates before setting down bowls of chilled avocado soup along with glasses of a light chardonnay. He watched in rapt fascination as Marissa enjoyed a spoonful of the soup, the way her eyes closed in pleasure and her tongue darted out to catch the bit on her lip. He was immediately envious of her tongue, wishing it was his that was taking the drop away, before using that same tongue to part her lips and plunder her mouth, drowning in her sweetness.

"What? Is there something on my lip?" Marissa

asked. She gently patted the area Donovan was staring at with her napkin.

"No."

"Oh."

Donovan forced his eyes away from her lips by taking a deliberate spoonful of soup. The moment, filled with unspoken this and unnamed that, came with a type of energy that seemed to settle in the room. For the first time Marissa was aware of light jazz playing in the background. Had it always been there or was this music inside her head, played from heartstrings being pulled in various directions?

"The land has been in the family for generations," Donovan offered after a couple sips of soup. "It's a long story, but the short of it is that during the gold rush, my adventurous ancestor, Nicodemus, came west with the Drakes of Louisiana. During the trip his master, who was more like a brother since the two had grown up together, almost died. Nicodemus saved his life and the family was so grateful that they willed him this portion of land."

"Wow, that's amazing. And he had the foresight to start a vineyard?"

"No, that was my great-grandfather's vision."

"Ah, yes, I remember now. Papa Dee. His story is in the room's welcome brochure. He was born in the house on the hill as I recall, what has become the honeymoon suite."

"You recall correctly."

"You must be proud to have such a rich family history."

"I am." Donovan nodded. "My family has worked hard to do right by this land. That's probably one of the reasons that I take the work so seriously. Maybe it's just my personality, maybe it's because I'm the oldest in this generation, but I feel the weight of the Drake legacy on my shoulders."

Marissa noted that his shoulders looked broad enough to carry the load. "From what I've seen so far it appears that you're doing an awesome job."

"I try." Donovan finished his soup and pushed the bowl away as he sat back. "I remember your telling Mama that you have a brother, correct?"

"Yes, it's just the two of us."

"Older, correct?"

"Yes, by three years, and married. They are expecting their second child."

"Congratulations." The ever-observant Donovan noticed Marissa's slight change of mood. Figuring that he could guess the cause of it, he decided to go ahead and venture down the road. "What about you? Are marriage and kids on the horizon?"

"Like yesterday, if my mother has her say."

"Ha! Is her name Genevieve?"

"No, it's Yolanda. But like yours, my mother is chomping at the bit for me to be married, almost pushing me down the aisle."

"Ha! Boy, do I know that feeling. She's been trying to marry me off since I turned twenty-five."

"I'd have figured someone like you would be married already."

"Who's someone like me?"

Marissa cocked her head as she pondered the answer. "Unlike your brother, who is a big ol' playboy, you seem more serious, more focused. I don't know. You don't strike me as the club-going guy with dozens of random phone numbers stashed on your phone. Of course, I could be totally wrong about you but—"

"No, you're nailing it on the head pretty good."

"It's not a bad thing," Marissa hurriedly continued, lest Donovan take offense to what she'd just said. They were having such a cordial moment she didn't want to spoil it. "In fact, it's refreshing to talk with someone who isn't trying to hit on me every other sentence."

"I was just getting around to that."

His face was serious, but Marissa detected the twinkle in his eye. She was starting to see the human that lived behind the stuffed shirt that walked around the office. And she was very much liking what she saw. So much so that she decided to be honest and share her very limited love experience.

"I grew up in a loving but sheltered environment. Great for building feelings of security, not so great in developing an eye for choosing the right man. I met my first real boyfriend in college. He was not only domineering and verbally abusive, but unfaithful, as well."

"Damn."

"I know, quite the trifecta. During those first six months he was charming, protective. That's how I saw it. What I thought was consideration for my well-being was actually control. By the time I'd figured that out, I'd already been in the relationship a year and was hopelessly in love. My first time out the gate and that was my love experience. Left me quite traumatized, as you can imagine."

"Was that the guy you ran into that night? At the restaurant?"

"No. Like I've said, that man and I never dated. He was my best friend. At least that's what I thought...."

The brightness in her eyes dimmed, replaced with a sadness that Donovan immediately wanted to alleviate.

"We don't have to talk about him," he said.

"Thank you." They ate a few moments in silence. "What about you? Why aren't you married?"

"We don't have to talk about that either," was Donovan's dry reply.

Marissa chuckled. "Touché. But you seem like a good person, and you come from a good family." Sitting back she eyed him, as if giving him due consideration. "I think you'll get married one day," she concluded.

Donovan looked at her, his expression unreadable. "Yes," he said at last. "Maybe one day."

Chapter 13

By the time dinner had ended, Marissa felt she and Donovan were less like strangers and more like associates who one day just might be friends. Along with preferring jazz to hip-hop, wine to hard liquor and summer climates to winter snows, a love for business was also common ground. Marissa was finally understanding Donovan's wry sense of humor. When they left the restaurant and walked into the picture-perfect night, with its star-filled velvety blue sky and gentle breeze, she could tell that neither was ready for the evening to end.

"I'd ask if you'd like to go for a walk, but those shoes don't look too comfortable."

"Are you saying you don't like my heels?" Marissa teased. Another thing she'd noticed and appreciated about Donovan was his directness. It was so unlike the glib tongues of most of the men she encountered, ready with endless compliments and come-ons meant to flatter and take her off guard.

"They're very nice. But they're what my mother calls 'sit down' shoes. As in, there are shoes you purchase to walk in and others that are meant to simply look good, that can take you from the door to a chair. Those look like the latter."

"Your mother is a wise woman. If you give me two minutes, I can change my shoes and would love to go for a walk. That chocolate lava cake was sinful, and I think I can already feel it wrapping around my thighs."

Less than ten minutes later, Marissa rejoined Donovan in the hotel lobby. She'd changed from her suit into an ankle-length dress with a floral design and flat sandals. Donovan had removed his jacket. As they exited the restaurant into the warm night, he rolled up his shirt sleeves. They began walking along a cobbled path that led through one herb garden, then another floral one and on to a pond and waterfall about half a mile away. Theirs was a companionable silence, enjoying the sights and sounds of the evening as each waded through a myriad of thoughts.

"His name is Steven," Marissa said at last.

"Huh?"

"The man who was at the bar that night. His name is Steven. We met in college and became best friends." Donovan, as if sensing the delicacy of the moment, remained silent. She continued, "I met him during my first day of classes and since it was my first time really away from home his friendly, carefree personality was just what I needed. I'm more of an introvert by nature, normally more comfortable surrounded by those I know and who know me. My parents were overly protective of me and my brother, me mostly, so when I went off to college my experience with men in particular was limited. I hadn't even had a boyfriend." Marissa glanced at Donovan to gauge his reaction, but his face was a mask. "Steven was a sophomore and he showed me the ropes, where everything was and who to watch out for."

"He didn't try to date you?"

"He did, but I just wasn't feeling him like that. He always felt more like my brother. In fact, he even reminded me of Timothy."

"Timothy is your brother?"

Marissa nodded. "He started dating someone, and I met Joseph, the guy I told you about at dinner, the controlling, serial cheater...my first boyfriend. Even though his girlfriend never liked me, Steven and I continued to be friends. He never liked Joseph either and told me so, but I was too caught up to listen. Leaving him was the one piece of advice from Steven that I wish I'd heeded. I should have left him after the first affair, and definitely after finding out he'd fathered a child. Things look very different when you're eighteen."

"You shouldn't be so hard on yourself. We've all made bad relationship choices, especially during the teens and twenties. We barely know ourselves. And what you were dealing with? That had to be a hard situation. Especially at such a young age."

"Yes, and especially considering it was my first experience with relationships. My self-esteem took a pounding." They reached a bench on the far side of the pond. Marissa sat down. Donovan joined her. "Not long after breaking up with Joseph, I met another man."

Again, that look of sadness that Donovan wanted to permanently erase. "What happened with him?" His voice was soft, filled with compassion. When she remained silent, he prodded, "Another cheater?"

Her smile was wistful in response. "Yes, he found another woman, one that I definitely couldn't compete with." She looked at Donovan. "Her name was cocaine."

"I'm so sorry, Marissa."

"Me, too. Except for the addiction, he was a good guy." A helicopter could be heard in the distance. The two became quiet as they scoured the sky, finally spotting the blinking red light just behind them. As it continued its southerly journey toward San Diego, Marissa continued, "Anyway, after putting that relationship behind me, I decided to focus on work. Steven and I became close friends again."

"You'd grown apart?"

"His girlfriend had convinced him to end our friendship, which he did, until they broke up."

Donovan's eyes were thoughtful as he looked into the distance. "Being that he was such a good friend to you, it's interesting that you didn't date."

"He felt the same way." Donovan noticed the tightness in her voice, but when he looked over, Marissa had regained control of whatever emotion his comment had evoked. "But I was never physically attracted to him. And with my second breakup happening so quickly after the first one, I was over men, period. I needed a break."

Donovan nodded his understanding. "So by now you'd graduated college?"

"Yes, and lucky for me, Steven was climbing the corporate ladder at a technology company. He told me about a job opening and I ended up working at the same company, though in a different department. He seemed to be okay with the fact that I said I wasn't interested, and our friendship continued."

"He seemed to be okay with it, huh? Obviously something happened that proved otherwise."

Marissa nodded. "The night he took me out for my birthday."

"What happened then?" Donovan asked, leaning forward slightly to catch Marissa's soft-spoken words.

"He tried to r—" She cleared her throat. "He put something in my drink."

"He drugged you?"

"That was his plan. He and I were drinking at the bar and when I left to use the restroom, a couple seated next to us saw him put something in my drink. When I came back, they told me."

"And you believed them."

"I did."

"Why?"

"Because after using the restroom," Marissa said as she looked out across the pond, "we were supposed to go to his house. He'd said he had something to show me. It was the timing and the look on his face when the couple told me what he'd done. He vehemently denied it but my intuition told me they were telling the truth."

"Marissa." Donovan's voice was filled with compassion and something else. "I'm sorry about what happened to you. I know what it's like to be betrayed—how much it hurts. I've been there." Marissa looked at him in surprise. "Yes."

"What happened?"

Donovan looked at his watch. "Maybe I'll tell you one of these days."

"It sounds like when it comes to broken hearts, you know exactly what I mean."

"It took a while, but I'm over the hurt that my ex caused me. My problem right now is timing. Lately work is the only woman I'm dating. And speaking of, I've got a seven o'clock breakfast meeting in the morning. I'm going to call it a night."

He walked her back to the hotel lobby and saw her safely to the elevator doors. He returned to his parents' home and was glad to see the house quiet. There was too much on his mind to feel like talking to anyone. He prepared for the following day and took a shower in an effort to calm down his body from hours of inhaling Marissa's scent. He lay down, but could not fall asleep.

As was always the case when there was a project before him, his mind whirled, continually breaking down what needed to be accomplished into manageable portions and then figuring out the most effective way to proceed. That is what kept him awake at this moment, running various scenarios to accomplish his end goal. He tossed and turned, and as the beginnings of sleep finally overcame him he was satisfied with the strategy now taking shape. He'd told Marissa that there were good men out there. *You've got nine days to get in those panties.* But that's not how Donovan saw it. He figured he had nine days, no, eight now, to show her just what a good man looked like.

Chapter 14

Donovan pulled into his reserved parking space just before eight o'clock. He'd awakened to a text saying that the Wednesday morning breakfast meeting with San Diego's African American Chamber of Commerce had been canceled due to an emergency with the president of that organization's family. But rather than turn over for a few more winks, he'd gotten out of bed, showered and enjoyed breakfast with Papa Dee, the only family member who'd been stirring at that time of day. He felt good, relaxed, as if a load had been lifted. The cause, of course, was Marissa and the wonderful time they'd had last night. The corner they'd turned, the new path of friendship they'd traveled. His heart was smiling, and as Donovan neared the executive offices he wondered if he'd ever felt like this before.

Entering the break room, Donovan was surprised

to see the coffee machine on with pots of java and hot water all ready. It was a rare day that somebody beat him to work. Thinking that maybe in Diamond's absence one of the marketing assistants had decided to begin work on the fall campaign, he headed toward the PR and marketing arm of the company. On his way he passed the filing room, and he stopped when he saw a shard of light from under the door.

"Good morning, Jo—" he began. At the vision in front of him, the words died on his lips. It wasn't Jodie combing through past marketing pieces as he'd assumed but Marissa, seated on the floor with several files around her, going through the archived company photos he'd told her about last night, hundreds that had yet to be scanned into the computer, a back-burner project for the next intern. She didn't notice him at first. A closer look that revealed earbuds and her slightly bobbing head provided the explanation. He took advantage of the unguarded moment and noticed how an errant strand of hair followed the curve of her jaw and rested alongside her slender neck, the one he'd imagined running his lips across and tongue against. In the few days she'd worked there, he realized this loose ponytail on top of the head was her go-to style. He liked it, too, sort of like her personality, on the quiet, conservative side but with a bit of devil-may-care to show that life shouldn't be taken too seriously.

Today she wore jeans, the low-riding kind. Her top was a simple printed number, and when she leaned forward to place a picture back in its file, he saw the strings of the pink thong she wore. There was pink in the print of her top, as well. Donovan smiled his approval at her aesthetic awareness. And again that hint at flirtatiousness, a carefree, girly-girl side.

To her right, against the wall, was a pair of wedge sandals, Donovan guessed three or four inches high. No wonder she was barefoot as she sat cross-legged on the floor. Who could reach the floor without breaking something in those towering things? Her toes were nice, too, he decided, painted in a respectful and corporate-conscious color of beige. He wanted to rub her feet, kiss her toes. He wanted to make intimate acquaintance with every area between there and those loose tendrils down the side of her face. His manhood twitched, growing hard at the ready. Donovan forced his thoughts elsewhere, took a long deep breath and reminded himself of his plan: to show Marissa the face of a good man.

He walked over and lightly squeezed her shoulder. Marissa jumped, saw that it was him and closed her eyes in relief. Pulling the earbuds out of her ear, she reached over and paused the iPod, as well. "You scared me," she said breathily, placing a hand to her chest before standing. "I came in to look through these archives, not expecting anyone here until eight-thirty. That's when Kat told me most of the employees arrived."

"My business breakfast was canceled," Donovan replied, his voice low, his eyes drawn to her mouth, as they often were, before slowly traveling back up to her almond-shaped, almost black orbs, with just a hint of a twinkle that came with her smile. "Good morning."

Marissa chuckled, part nervousness, part nana tingling. "Good morning."

"You're here early."

"Yes, I woke up before the alarm went off, thinking about the stories you'd told me about your family and how this vineyard came to be. I find it fascinating. When I couldn't get back to sleep, I decided to come in and check out these pictures you told me about." She walked over to one, showing three young children, two boys in cowboy getups and a girl in a frilly gingham frock, each holding a cluster of grapes. "This one is adorable, Donovan. But you and Dexter as cowboys? Really?"

Donovan laughed as he walked over to where Marissa stood. He knew exactly which picture she held, remembered where and when it had been taken as if it were yesterday. "Girl, I'll have you know that there's not a red-blooded boy alive who hasn't wanted to be a cowboy at one point or another in his life. That's if he knows what a cowboy is. My cousins in Louisiana are all excellent horsemen. I don't do too bad myself."

"You ride horses?" She asked the question with the same incredulity as if she'd asked, "You just returned from the moon?"

"Ha! Yes, baby, all of the Drakes know how to ride."

He hadn't meant to call her baby, hadn't meant for the meaning of his sentence to contain such…heat. But with one offhand comment, a fire had started. He could see it blazing in Marissa's eyes and knew that if he didn't do something, like now, to tamp the flames, he'd make love to her right here on the file room floor. "Come with me."

Marissa, with images of Donovan riding still dancing in her head, was caught off guard as Donovan placed a firm grasp on her arm and began walking over to where her shoes were lined toe-first against the wall. "Where are we going?" she asked breathlessly.

"I want to take you on a quick tour of the vineyard."

He felt the heat from the arm he still held and quickly dropped it. But not before memorizing the silkiness of her skin and the faint hint of flowers that seemed a permanent part of all things Marissa.

"Are you sure we have time to do that now? There's still so much work to do."

"There will always be work," Donovan said, quoting his grandfather, David, Jr. "But it's a beautiful day, and since you're playing such a part in the expanding of the Drake brand, I think it's time you see firsthand how everything happens."

Marissa had put on her wedge heels and her head now reached above his shoulder. She was insanely aware of him as they walked down the hall—the seriousness of his countenance, so unlike his playful brother's, the musky smell of his cologne, the purposefulness in his stride. They went out a back door, next to where several golf carts sat parked and ready. "Can you get in?" Donovan asked, looking skeptically at Marissa's heels.

"Ha! I've worn heels since I was twelve years old," she responded, easily hopping into the passenger seat of the late-model cart. "I can run track in these things."

"Ha!"

He started the cart and soon they were rolling across the immaculately manicured grasslands, off the beaten path. Instead of heading toward the hotel, with the stand-alone wine shop and cellar across the street, Donovan was taking them toward the vineyards, with Papa Dee's Suite, the home Donovan's ancestors had built, sitting majestically on the hill beyond. Marissa held on to the door and took in the scene, glad for the quiet and a moment to both settle her mind and rein in her feelings for Donovan.

"I read the story about that house," she said after a moment, pointing to the white house on the hill with the slate red roof. "That was a beautiful story."

"Yes, Nicodemus Drake was one heck of a man. Built that place alongside some of his neighbors at a time when owning land wasn't always easy. I have the utmost respect for those men who came along in the nineteenth century, when life was hard and short. They paved the way for our success. I never forget that. Another reason I guess that for me, life is not a game."

"Do you take after him?"

Donovan cut an eye over at Marissa to see if she was joking, but her expression was totally serious. "I'd like to think I do," he said with a shrug. "But Daddy says I'm more like my grandfather, David Drake, Jr. Dexter takes after Papa Dee, not only in his love for wine-making, but also in his crazy personality."

"Your brother does seem to have a zest for life."

"Yes, he does. I do, too," he added as an afterthought.

"I can see that." When Donovan looked doubtful, she continued, "Really, I can. I've observed you with your family, your mother especially, at the engagement party and the wedding, too. You don't show it much, but there's a fun, softer side to you."

"Oh, so you've been checking me out on the low, huh?"

"Please." She smiled and didn't deny what he said. "What about your sister, Diamond? Who do you think she takes after?"

"She's probably more like Daddy, but she has some of Mama's ways, too. But, then again, Papa Dee says that she has ways like his wife, my great-grandmother Luella."

"Did you know her?"

Donovan nodded. "She died five years ago, at the age of eighty-nine."

"Ah, so Papa Dee was rolling with a younger woman!"

"He's still trying to do that. Last time they took him to the casino he tried to talk to a woman who was seventy-five."

Marissa laughed, and to Donovan it sounded like magic, full and throaty yet light like fresh air. He could get used to hearing that laughter, he decided. In fact, when it came to him and thoughts about Marissa, he realized he could get used to a lot of things. For the next hour, he switched from family historian to tour conductor, showing Marissa the various plots and types of grapes, fermenting tanks, hoppers and presses. She was particularly fascinated with the storage area, the cellar, with its concrete walls that were several feet thick, and the oak barrels aging gallon upon gallon of wine. The coolness of the basement contrasted with the unspoken heat between Donovan and Marissa, ever present amid their innocent talk of vintages and wine types and growing up in Southern California.

By the time they returned to the office, the workday was in full swing. Donovan was immediately called into a meeting, one for which Marissa had taken information he'd given her and made impressive handouts. Marissa was busy replacing the pictures and folders left out during their impromptu vineyard tour before beginning her task of data entry. They didn't see each other for the rest of the day, but Donovan was never far from her mind.

As it turned out, she was never far from his mind either. It had taken discipline honed through years of work to stay focused and mentally present as one meeting had run into the next. His mind kept drifting back to the look on Marissa's face as they'd toured the grounds; her sparkling eyes and joyful laughter. The more he knew about her the more he wanted to know, and the more determined he became to find out.

Chapter 15

Donovan watched as Genevieve eyed him speculatively. They'd just gathered around the dining room table for a light supper. Donovan was sure his mother had made his childhood favorite, tuna casserole, just for him. It was the weekend, and even though it was a working one he'd wanted to spend the evening with Marissa. But she'd declined, saying that because they'd be working the next day she planned to make short use of the hotel's gym and then call it a night. So for Donovan, this was a quiet evening with Mom and Dad. Diamond and Jackson were still away, enjoying their honeymoon. Dexter was out on a date. And David, Sr., Junior and Mary had joined their senior group for bingo night at the casino. It was a rare dinner moment when he had his parents all to himself, a fact he found himself relishing almost as much as the fare in front of him. He sank his fork into another delicious forkful of gooey goodness: thick hunks of fresh tuna, sweet peas, thick egg noodles and an abundance of cheese, just the way he liked it.

"This is so good, Mama," he said, after swallowing the bite. "Reminds me of those sleepovers after Friday night football. All of the other guys would want tacos or burgers but even so, you'd make a whole casserole just for me."

"I think you got that from your Grandmother Mary," Genevieve replied, taking a much daintier bite of the salad she'd made to accompany the main course. "It's one of her favorite meals, as well." She continued to look at her son, the smile on her face turning into a chuckle as she watched the exuberance with which Donovan was finishing off his second helping. "I remember something else about those nights. You always were the first to finish eating," she gently admonished him. "You know, if Papa were here he'd remind you that the food isn't going anywhere."

"That's for sure," Donald said, scraping his fork across a cleaned plate in a nod to the chef's skills. "And if Mama were here she'd tell you to chew your food thoroughly to help aid your digestion."

"Well," Donovan said as he continued his hasty devouring of the food on his plate, "it's a good thing that they aren't here!"

"It's good to spend time with you, son." Donald wiped his mouth on a napkin and leaned back in his chair to observe his firstborn.

After taking a sip of tea, Genevieve commented, "You look happy."

Donovan didn't need to see a rod and reel to know when it was fishing season. "I am."

"Any particular reason?"

"Sure." Donovan finished his last bite and, after wiping his mouth, mirrored his dad's relaxed position. "Right now, about thirty million of them." That was the conservative projection from the Asian market over the next five years: thirty million dollars.

"You're talking about your ongoing meetings with the Asian businessmen." Genevieve didn't walk the corporate office halls, but she knew what was going on as if she did. Donovan nodded. "But that's not the meeting *I'm* talking about."

"Oh?"

"No, the meeting I'm talking about would have given you about thirty-six reasons to be happy."

Donovan shrugged. "I don't get it."

"Not yet, but you want to." Donovan's confused look caused both his parents to laugh. "Son," Genevieve said, placing her elbow on the table and her chin in her cupped hand. "I'm talking about that thirty-six, twenty-four, thirty-six you've been working with these past couple days."

"Ha!" Donald's eyes sparkled as he eyed his wife.

"Oh, man," Donovan groaned. "That one was pretty bad, Mama."

Donald winked at his wife. "Hmph. I thought it was pretty good." He continued laughing as Genevieve removed their dinner dishes and brought out dessert. "That was the two of you I saw the other morning, right? When your mom and I decided to change up our morning walk routine and go out by the vineyards?"

"You would decide to change courses that day," Donovan mumbled.

"I think she's a very pretty girl," Donald offered.

"How is she working out, Don, at the office?" Genevieve asked.

"Very good. She's smart," he quickly added, lest his mother get ideas.

"You know what happened the last time one of my children gave a tour of the vineyard."

"Enough already, Mama," Donovan warned, but it was halfhearted.

"Dating Jackson's assistant would definitely make life easier," Donald speculated. "Keeping it in the family so to speak."

"On that note," Donovan said, rising from the table. "I think I'll head back to the office. I want to go over the figures again before the next meeting with investors."

"What, no dessert?"

Donovan leaned down and kissed his mother on the forehead. "I'll get some later," he said before leaving, knowing exactly which particular sweetness he'd like to taste. Marissa had said she needed time for her heart to heal, but their recent interactions had given him greater hope that maybe, just maybe, he could make like a doctor and assist in her recovery.

Marissa walked down the winding staircase from the second-floor gym and spa area to the lobby. She'd just enjoyed a ninety-minute workout, due only in part to the baked potato with everything on it that she'd had for lunch. No, she told herself. She was really working out to try to get Donovan out of her system.

After working with him the past five days, there was no use denying what she felt. The attraction was definitely there. And, yes, she might even be really, like *really,* in like with him. She'd even go that far. Okay, she'd do him in a heartbeat if not for the complications. Problem number one: he was her boss's brother-in-law. What would happen if their time together ended badly? She pondered that while grabbing a bottle of sparkling water from the gift shop. And while he seemed genuine enough, what if he was one of those low-key players, acting all serious and aboveboard with a harem on the down low? She'd get her heart broken, that's what. Before knowing the truth, no one could have convinced her that her ex, Joseph, had multiple women and children to boot. Just because a man didn't seem like a womanizer, didn't mean he didn't have dozens of prospects at the ready.

The whole situation seemed impossible, which made Marissa wonder why she was considering it at all. If things didn't work out between them, she'd still certainly have to see Donovan from time to time. At the very least she'd see his sister, Diamond, on occasion. Wouldn't that be a constant reminder of what she couldn't have, of what could never be? *And just what do you want, Marissa?* If she were truthful, she'd admit to wanting to throw caution to the wind, forget her past heartbreaks and give Donovan a chance. To go on a couple dates at least, test the waters and all that good stuff. *But what about Steven?* This time at the resort was giving her the chance to almost forget about that little problem. But past experience was more than enough proof that her ex-best friend wasn't going to simply go away.

Marissa entered her suite and immediately saw that a cream-colored envelope had been slid underneath her door in her absence. Her heartbeat quickened immediately. *Donovan*. She picked up the single piece of Drake Wines Resort and Spa stationery and read the typed note:

> *Dear Ms. Hayes:*
> *Thank you for all of your hard work. The suc-*
> *cess of this week's meetings was in part due to*
> *you. Please enjoy the enclosed certificate, and*
> *this evening, with my compliments.*
> *Thinking of you,*
> *Donovan*

The note was short, but Marissa still read it three times. She looked at the certificate and read the note again. What did it mean? Not the certificate, it was self-explanatory: one full-body massage in the privacy of her suite. But by whom? Him? Marissa felt herself grow wet at the thought. Without even thinking about it, she began stripping and headed to the shower. Once inside, with the water pouring over her body, other thoughts poured in as well, thoughts of her ex-boyfriend, Joseph, and how assumptive he always was that she'd be where he wanted her to be and do what he'd say. *But Donovan's not like that, Marissa. You know he isn't.*

"Right, that isn't Donovan," she told herself, soaping her body with her favorite scent: a mix of citrus and vanilla. She ran her hands over her body, across her breasts. Closed her eyes and tweaked her nipples, imagining Donovan's hands. How long had it been since someone else had touched her? *Too long.* She turned and let the water run down the curve of her back, bent over and felt the warm spray on her round booty. Her hands followed the water: cheeks, thighs, stomach, the valley of paradise. Realizing the time, she caught herself. Fully turned on, she was ready, anxious, giddy with Donovan's creative seduction.

Exiting the shower, she dried off, scanned her closet of limited choices and after noticing the fluffy white robe the hotel provided, donned it instead. The plush fabric felt soft against her bare skin, and she imagined simply letting it fall when Donovan entered and brazenly claiming his lips in a kiss. *Naughty girl.* It was only fitting. Before the evening was over, Marissa intended to not only get naughty, but to get downright nasty.

She heard a knock at the door. Taking a deep breath to calm the butterflies, she walked over and looked through the peep hole.

Her heart sank.

It wasn't Donovan.

"Good evening, Ms. Drake," the Asian woman said, bowing slightly. "We are here for your full-body massage.

"Oh."

"Did you not receive the invitation?"

Marissa realized how her less-than-enthusiastic response must have sounded. It wasn't the masseuse's fault that her fantasy had not played out. She forced a smile and answered. "Yes, I received it. Please, come in."

The woman wheeled in a portable table, followed by another woman who pulled in a product-filled case. "We are told that you are a very special guest and that we must take special care of you. We'd like to set up here, in the living room area, if that's all right."

Marissa hadn't intended for her sigh to be audible.

"Are you sure there is no problem?" the lead masseuse asked, deep concern instantly on her face. "It is possible to reschedule, if you'd like."

"No, uh, no," Marissa countered, lifting her chin in an attempt to save face. "None at all."

"Good! This session will last two full hours. Let us begin."

Chapter 16

Even though it was Saturday and she probably could have come in later, Marissa still left her suite at 8:25 a.m. for the short trip to the executive offices. She figured with it being a weekend, she wouldn't encounter that many Drake employees. She even wondered if she and Donovan would be the only ones in the office.

Immediately her mind went to things she'd love to do when alone with him but she shifted those thoughts. If she hadn't been sure Donovan was interested in her before last night, she definitely knew it now. Had it been any other man, a massage invitation would have been a barely veiled if not blatant precursor to a night of intimacy.

But the invitation Donovan sent said she'd get a massage. And that's exactly what had happened. A man of his word. Another rare quality in her limited male experience.

So why was she mad at him? Because he hadn't acted like the men she knew, like Joseph or Steven? And she'd wanted him to. Sure, the massage had been perfection, left her as limp as a wet noodle. But the experience, especially his kind gesture, had left her with a void that needed to be filled. Last night had left Marissa wanting Donovan more than she'd ever wanted any man.

Before now, sex had been something she could take or leave, something she rarely thought of. But she'd tossed and turned all night, had squeezed her legs together in an attempt to quell the throbbing ache, the relentless longing that burned between her thighs, a longing that she had a feeling only one man could fulfill. Sleep had stayed at bay until the wee hours of the morning and the body that had been so relaxed and nurtured the night before was now wound tight as a drum. So yes, Marissa was angry at Donovan for making her want him and angry at herself for her lack of mental restraint.

She reached the executive offices and used the temporary card she'd been given to unlock the door. The delicious aroma of coffee hit her as soon as she entered, a sign that even as early as she was, someone was earlier. She'd hoped to arrive before Donovan, give herself a moment to don a professional veneer to face him. With any luck, it would be one of the accountants she encountered or another of the assistants in to catch up.

Unlike during the week, the reception area was dim, the offices at the front darkened and locked. She turned down the hallway on her right, bypassing the file room and entering the finance area. She realized at once that luck was not on her side. There, in all of his masculine glory, was Donovan, somehow looking professional

even though he was dressed in jeans, a polo shirt and…
what? Cowboy boots? Marissa was immediately reminded of Donovan's statement the other night, that all
of the Drakes knew how to ride. Looking at him now,
six feet of dark butterscotch, broad shoulders and thick
thighs, she just bet he did. His hip leaned against her
desk as he casually thumbed through the mail stacked
in the inbox. It was almost as though he'd been waiting for her.

*There you go again, Marissa. Stop acting like a love-
struck fool. Donovan is interested in your business, not
bedroom skills. Get yourself together!*

He looked up and that subtle smile that she'd come
to recognize and look forward to scampered across
his face before being replaced with a less discern-
ible expression. "Good morning." He stood straight as
she walked toward him, catching her gaze before she
quickly turned her face away and walked around him,
placing her purse in the desk drawer. "It is a good morning, isn't it?"

"It is a beautiful morning," Marissa assured him,
trying very hard to match his good mood. "An angel
gifted me with a spa treatment last night. It was heavenly." Having put down her purse and somewhat shaped
her expression into one of gratitude instead of chagrin,
she turned to face him. "Thank you."

"So you enjoyed it?" He leaned against the desk and
immediately Marissa took in his familiar scent. "Your
stiff demeanor had me worried for a minute, thought I
might have to fire some workers for not properly doing
their job."

"No, the massage was wonderful. It's just that afterward, well…"

"Well, what?"

Marissa shrugged, realizing that she may be revealing too much and wondering why she cared so much. "I didn't sleep well."

Donovan frowned. "Lei did the massage?" Marissa nodded. "Most clients say that after she's done with them they sleep like a baby."

"I guess I had a lot on my mind."

"Care to share?"

"No," was her quick reply. "I'm ready to get down to business so tomorrow I can spend my day off in San Diego, go to church and then go by my apartment to check on things. We are still at a point where I can take tomorrow off, correct?" Donovan nodded. "Good. If we end the day early enough, I'll drive down there tonight."

"Okay. After you get settled then come into my office."

As Donovan watched her grab a coffee cup and leave, he frowned. Something was wrong. But what? He thought that the massage would relax Marissa, have her feeling loose and carefree. Instead the opposite seemed to have happened and she seemed more uptight than ever.

He walked back into his office, still consumed with what could be bothering Marissa. Was it Steven, the jerk who'd tried to assault her and left her so distrusting of men? Had he contacted her, threatened her somehow? Or maybe it was another man. Yes, she'd said that her focus was work, and yes she'd said she was taking a break from dating. But Donovan could see someone who looked like Marissa spending only so many nights alone. He walked over to the window, seeking the peace that usually surrounded him when he gazed upon the

KIMANI
ROMANCE

An Important
Message from
the Publisher

Dear Reader,

Because you've chosen to read one of our fine novels, I'd like to say "thank you"! And, as a special way to say thank you, I'm offering to send you two more Kimani™ Romance novels and two surprise gifts— absolutely FREE! These books will keep it real with true-to-life African American characters that turn up the heat and sizzle with passion.

Please enjoy the free books and gifts with our compliments...

Glenda Howard
For Kimani Press™

Peel off Seal and
Place Inside...

EDITOR'S
FREE GIFT
SEAL
THANK YOU

Wᵉ'd like to send you two free books to introduce you t
Kimani™ Romance books. These novels feature strong
sexy women, and African-American heroes that are charming
loving and true. Our authors fill each page with exceptiona
dialogue, exciting plot twists, and enough sizzling romanc
to keep you riveted until the very end!

KIMANI ROMANCE...LOVE'S ULTIMATE DESTINATION

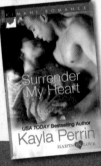

Your two books h
combined cover ʳ
of $12.50 in the U
$14.50 in Canada,
are yours **FREE!**

We'll even send yᵉ
two wonderful
surprise gifts.
You can't lose!

2 FREE BONUS GIFTS!

*We'll send you two wonderful surprise gifts,
(worth about $10) absolutely FREE, just for
giving KIMANI™ ROMANCE books a try! Don't
miss out—MAIL THE REPLY CARD TODAY!*

Visit us online at
www.ReaderService.cᵒ

THE EDITOR'S "THANK YOU" FREE GIFTS INCLUDE:

➤ Two Kimani™ Romance Novels
➤ Two exciting surprise gifts

YES! I have placed my Editor's "thank you" Free Gifts seal in the space provided at right. Please send me 2 FREE Books, and my 2 FREE Mystery Gifts. I understand that I am under no obligation to purchase anything further, as explained on the back of this card.

PLACE
FREE GIFTS
SEAL
HERE

168/368 XDL FTF5

Please Print

FIRST NAME

LAST NAME

ADDRESS

APT.#   CITY

STATE/PROV.   ZIP/POSTAL CODE

Thank You!

Offer limited to one per household and not applicable to series that subscriber is currently receiving.

Your Privacy—The Reader Service is committed to protecting your privacy. Our Privacy Policy is available online at www.ReaderService.com or upon request from the Reader Service. We make a portion of our mailing list available to reputable third parties that offer products we believe may interest you. If you prefer that we not exchange your name with third parties, or if you wish to clarify or modify your communication preferences, please visit us at www.ReaderService.com/consumerchoice or write to us at Reader Service Preference Service, P.O. Box 9062, Buffalo, NY 14269. Include your complete name and address.

The Reader Service - Here's How It Works:

Accepting your 2 free books and 2 free gifts (gifts valued at approximately $10.00) places you under no obligation to buy anything. You may keep the books and gifts and return the shipping statement marked "cancel." If you do not cancel, about a month later we'll send you 4 additional books and bill you just $4.94 each in the U.S. or $5.49 each in Canada. That is a savings of at least 21% off the cover price. Shipping and handling is just 50¢ per book in the U.S. and 75¢ per book in Canada.* You may cancel at any time, but if you choose to continue, every month we'll send you 4 more books, which you may either purchase at the discount price or return to us and cancel your subscription. *Terms and prices subject to change without notice. Prices do not include applicable taxes. Sales tax applicable in N.Y. Canadian residents will be charged applicable taxes. Offer not valid in Quebec. All orders subject to credit approval. Credit or debit balances in a customer's account(s) may be offset by any other outstanding balance owed by or to the customer. Offer available while quantities last. Books received may not be as shown. Please allow 4 to 6 weeks for delivery.

If offer card is missing write to: The Reader Service, P.O. Box 1867, Buffalo, NY 14240-1867 or visit www.ReaderService.com

BUSINESS REPLY MAIL
FIRST-CLASS MAIL   PERMIT NO. 717   BUFFALO, NY

POSTAGE WILL BE PAID BY ADDRESSEE

THE READER SERVICE
PO BOX 1867
BUFFALO NY 14240-9952

NO POSTAGE
NECESSARY
IF MAILED
IN THE
UNITED STATES

hundreds of acres that held the Drake name. His shoulders relaxed somewhat but the scowl remained. How did he unlock this mystery that was Marissa Hayes?

He realized that with all of his academic knowledge and corporate experience, in matters of the heart he was severely lacking. Unlike his brother, Donovan hadn't majored in women for the last ten years. Sure he'd had his share of one-night stands, had made the rounds in college as he honed his lover skills. Most of the time, there was little he had to do for these favors. Women seemed to flock to the silent, brooding type, as he'd been labeled. More often than not, women had been the aggressor in his many liaisons. That was fine with him. Like any Drake, he had a ferocious sexual appetite and loved women. But he'd never thought much about marriage, and when he did, he thought of his parents and grandparents, believing that if he ever did take that walk down the aisle it would be with someone he could envision spending a lifetime with.

He thought he'd met that woman seven years ago, when he was twenty-five. He'd believed Erica Kimble was the one who'd give him the kind of love that Luella had given Papa Dee, that Mary gave David, Jr., and that his mother, Genevieve, gave his father. Instead, she'd taken one of the most precious things a man can have away. That had happened almost two years ago and truth be told, Donovan had yet to fully recover.

"I'm ready." Marissa stood in his office a few steps from his desk. She was holding her mug and looking at him with a curious expression. He'd been so deep in thought that he hadn't heard her come in.

"Uh, yeah." Donovan placed his current thoughts to the side and reached for his laptop. "Now that we've inputted the business contacts, it's time to start the fun stuff," he said, clicking on some keys and reaching for a large accordion folder at the same time. "Inputting the wealthy potential customers who we'll invite to a series of exclusive parties to taste our wine. All of these contacts, and their detailed personal and company information, must be transferred into the database." He handed Marissa the weighty file.

"My goodness," she said after opening it up. "There's a lot."

"The most influential bankers, business owners and entrepreneurs from Beijing to Hong Kong," Donovan replied with a hint of pride. "My counterparts have been busy, and we need to have all of their information inputted as soon as possible, hopefully before making my next scheduled trip."

"You've been to China?"

"Seven times in the past six months."

"I'd love to go there. It seems so exotic."

"It's a beautiful country," Donovan replied, rising. "Listen, I have to run back to the house for a bit. There's something I need to take care of. Hit me up on my cell if you need me."

"Oh, okay." Marissa noted Donovan's rather abrupt departure. What did he have to go back to the house for when he'd just gotten to the office?

Chapter 17

Donovan jumped into his Mercedes for the short drive to the Drake estate. So far he'd handled Marissa as he would any project in which he envisioned success; he thought he'd mapped out a fairly good strategy. But due to his limited expertise in the area of females, things were not going as planned. It was time to do what he would have had this been any other type of business situation: call for backup.

He reached the house and strode purposefully into the great room. A surprised Genevieve turned from the plant she was watering. "Donovan! Did you forget something?"

"No, just need to holler at Dad a minute."

"He's with your grandfather. You'd better hurry though, I think they're leaving for the golf course."

"Thanks, Mama," Donovan said over his shoulder,

already heading to the front door. Donald was with David, Jr.? Perfect. Because when it came to Drake business two heads were better than one, and when it came to women three heads were better than two.

Donovan reached his dad and grandfather just as they were exiting the former spacious guest home where David and Mary now resided. Both men wore lightweight, knee-length shorts, cotton shirts and golf caps, and each had a large leather golf bag hoisted over his shoulder.

"Did you change your mind about working today?" Donald said as soon as Donovan exited his vehicle. "We'll wait on you if you'd like to grab your clubs and join us."

Donovan reached the two men. "I thought Dexter was supposed to join you two this morning?" Donald gave him a look, one that Donovan interpreted as Dexter doing his usual, getting sidetracked by a pretty face. He laughed. "All right, I got it. And I appreciate the invite, but I'm working. I just have a bit of a problem I need help with."

David and Donald were immediately all ears. They set their clubs down. "Do we need to go back inside?" Donald pointed toward the house. "Chef made a spinach frittata, and there's still some left."

"No, this needs to be a man-to-man conversation."

"All right, son. Let's walk down the path a bit."

The men walked and Donovan talked: about his attraction to Marissa, her hesitancy in dating men in general and her adamancy and reasons for not crossing the professional line with him in particular. "Dexter was right," he finished, having gone on for the better part of ten minutes. "What I'm feeling for Marissa isn't like what I've had for other women. She's different. I don't want to disrespect her by going against her wishes, but I don't want to take the chance of her getting away. I'm afraid that when Boss and Diamond get back from their trip, and she goes back to the construction company, that'll be it. She won't see me again."

A look passed between David and Donald, and there was a twinkle in his eye as David spoke. "Sounds like the real thing, son," he said simply.

"What?"

"You're in love with her, boy. Any blind man can see that. Same as how I felt when I saw Mary all those years ago, doing the Lindy Hop at Small's Paradise Club in Harlem."

Donovan smiled at the reference; he'd heard the story of this famed meeting for the first time when he was about ten years old and he never tired of hearing it. The smile was short-lived. Being in love looked good on other people, but given the one time he'd totally given his heart to somebody, he didn't think that he wore it too well.

"Look, Donovan." It was Donald's turn to add his two cents to the conversation. They'd neared a grove of full-grown palm trees that had been transported from Mexico and planted during the renovation. It formed a cove of sorts, as if it had been there for hundreds of years instead of barely one. Donald leaned against the tree, speaking casually, purposely, to try and calm his older son's fears. "I'll tell you like Daddy told me all those years ago when Genevieve was trying to act like she didn't want to give me the time of day. He reminded me of how it was for us to break horses. You remember those summers with your cousins in Louisiana, how they'd coax that filly into warming up to them, nudging them bit by bit until they could saddle the mare?"

"Geez, Daddy," Donovan said, the visuals conjured up from Donald's words could almost make a black man blush. David, Jr., laughed, obviously enjoying Donovan's rare show of discomfort.

"Son, you've got to saddle the filly before you can ride her, and you've got to ride her, make sure you fit, before you make her your own." Sensing how hard this was for his son, Donald hid his smile behind a cough, sobered his face and continued, "How much longer is Marissa in the office?"

"Not long enough," Donovan said, cursing what was usually one of his favorite holidays for showing up on the date it always did. He'd have gladly worked through it, but for the Drakes, the Fourth of July was a major holiday. Millions of dollars at stake or not, Genevieve had put her foot down and demanded he join the family for the annual festivities, their brunch at the very least. So, of course, he'd be there, and not demand that Marissa work while he did not. If he heeded his elders' advice and they gave him the right answers, next week he might produce some fireworks of his own. "I know I'm treating her with kid gloves. It's because I don't want to hurt her. From the look in her eyes, I can see that she's been through enough."

"Then keep being the man that I've taught you to be. Gentle, courteous, thoughtful, kind. Find out what she needs and give it to her before she needs it. Remember to make her feel like a woman who's worthy of your admiration and respect. You do all those things and you won't have to worry about what will happen when

Jackson gets back. Because whatever it is, you and her will be doing it together."

"In the meantime, get her in the saddle," Donald said with a chuckle as the men headed back up the path toward the house. "And before you go off with your wayward thinking, I'm talking about a real one. Take her riding, son. That trick has helped to wear down every filly that's gotten caught in the Drake crosshairs."

Fifteen minutes later, a more confident and completely determined Donovan strode back into the office. "Change of plans," he said as soon as he reached Marissa's desk. He didn't even glance at the massive amount of paperwork next to her computer, or the single-minded way in which she was rapidly clicking keys. "You need to go get changed. Put on a pair of jeans, a casual top and closed toe shoes."

"What's going on?" Marissa asked, still typing, eyes on the screen.

"I'm getting ready to take you riding."

Fingers stopped. Head snapped. Eyes widened. "As in on a horse?"

Unless you'd prefer another way, Donovan thought. "Of course," he said.

"I don't know about that," Marissa said slowly. The most she'd handled in the way of animals was Nippy, the family cocker spaniel. She'd loved him so much that they'd had a funeral, complete with procession and lights, when he'd died. Other than that, she'd never considered herself an animal lover. Aside from one grade-school outing, she'd never even visited the San Diego Zoo. "I'm not sure I'd like being on top of such a large animal." She blushed at the inference and quickly added, "I mean, I'm not too good around furry things." *Lord, please help me!*

Donovan laughed out loud, and the deep rumble felt like a warm breeze over Marissa's body. "I won't let anything happen to you," he insisted. "You'll be fine."

"What about work?"

"This is work. I'm going to show you some more of the Drake property and then introduce you to a very special Drake wine. Besides, I've noticed how fast you type. You'll whip through those stacks in no time."

Once again, Marissa thought, Donovan had done the unexpected and once again she was flying all over the place, sort of like the wispy hair of a dandelion following a child's heartfelt blow. "Who are you, Donovan Drake?" she asked under her breath, as she left to change clothes. "And what exactly are you doing to me?"

Chapter 18

Ten minutes later she was in the familiar golf cart, heading toward the house on the hill and then down the other side of it, to a piece of land she'd not seen before. The first thing she noticed was its tranquil beauty: a large expanse of green dotted with flowers, set against the backdrop of the coastal mountain range, embedded with boulders ranging from the size of apples to the size of cars. A large pond sat in the seat of a natural valley, and beyond it was a fenced-in area, encased with rough-hewn cedar planks secured with large nails and wires. At the very top of the slope, Donovan stopped the golf cart. They were silent as they looked out upon the massive expanse of land and profusion of colors.

And then she saw them. The horses, looking large and domineering even from this distance. Two were near a corner of the fence, facing each other as if in conversation. Another stood nearby, munching on grass. She turned her head and took in at least ten more, of various colors and in different poses. And then a rider in the distance, atop a horse whose coat was as black as night, its tail dancing behind him as he galloped across the field.

"This is beautiful," Marissa said, surprising herself by meaning the horses, as well. "All of this is Drake property?"

Donovan nodded. "As far as your eye can see." He started the cart and expertly navigated the uneven terrain until he came upon a barnlike structure next to the corral. They arrived at the same time as the horse and rider. The animal looked big from where she'd first seen him but here, up close and personal, he was huge! Marissa still thought he was beautiful. She also still believed that riding such a huge animal was, for her, a long shot.

"Let's go," Donovan said to her, hopping out of the cart as he spoke. The rider held up his hand in greeting. *"Hola, Diego,"* Donovan responded. *"Cómo estás, mi amigo?"*

"Bien, señor," Diego responded. *"Pero estará muy caliente más tarde, sí?"*

"Creo que sí," Donovan replied.

Marissa almost groaned. She'd never heard a foreign language sound so sexy. And that Donovan spoke it effortlessly? Who knew? The man was full of surprises, and so far she'd liked them all.

"I think we're in for a hot July and an even hotter August." He reached for Marissa, who was standing behind him, away from the horse. "Marissa," he said, gently guiding her forward by her elbow. "This is Diego, one of the finest horsemen in California. Diego, this is Boss's assistant, Marissa. She's helping me while he and my sister are gallivanting around the globe."

"Nice to meet you, *señorita*," Diego responded in heavily accented English. He offered a deeply tanned, calloused hand. The eyes in his weathered face were kind and the crow's-feet that appeared when he smiled seemed well earned. "Are you here to ride the horses?"

"Sí," Donovan replied before Marissa could consider an alternate answer.

"Perhaps I saddle for her Miss America. She is gentle, will take her time."

"Miss America?" Marissa queried despite her discomfort.

"Conceited little saddlebred," Donovan explained. "A light bay beauty, and she knows it."

"I don't want to ride her," Marissa said, shaking her head. "What if she takes off and I can't stop it?"

Donovan gave Marissa a patient look, a smile teasing the corners of his mouth.

Wait, is he enjoying this? "Is there something amusing about scaring me half to death?" she asked, forgetting her timidity.

"Don't worry. You'll ride with me," he said in response. He still held her arm and now casually rubbed his hand up and down it. The shiver Marissa felt had nothing to do with fear. "You'll be fine." This was delivered in a voice low yet firm, full of quiet authority and complete reassurance at the same time.

He walked over to the black stallion, a horse that Marissa felt towered over her but for whom Donovan seemed a perfect match. She watched as the horse eyed the man approaching, noticed him bob his head as if in greeting. Donovan rubbed the horse's nose and to her surprise began talking to him in Spanish. He rubbed his mane, then walked over to a bucket filled with carrots. He brought one over to the massive animal, who nibbled it right out of Donovan's hand.

"What's his name?" Marissa called out. For all her fear, there was something very likable about the big animals, something that seemed to draw her to them and become curious about their natures.

"Zephyr," Donovan said, still stroking the horse. "Fast as the wind. But I think we'd best ride Sauvignon," Donovan said to Diego, switching back to the horseman's native tongue. "Wait here," Donovan said to Marissa and then switched right back to Spanish as if he were a *vaquero verdadero*...a true Mexican cowboy.

The two men disappeared behind the wall of the barn and Marissa found herself alone, just her and Zephyr. The fence between them was a good five feet tall but it still seemed that the horse might be able to leap it with a good running start. They eyed each other warily, yet curiously, appearing to both take each other's measure. Zephyr took a step forward. Marissa took a step back. "Look, I don't want any trouble," she said nervously. Then, remembering how Donovan had conversed with the equine, she added, "Nothing personal," in a softer, kinder tone. "I'm just more comfortable when your kind is made of hard plastic and on a merry-go-round." Zephyr slowly batted his eyes, nodded once and swished his tail. Marissa's brow lifted in surprise. *Well, if I didn't know better...I'd think you understood me!*

While she was watching Zephyr turn and mosey down toward two gray horses, Donovan came back around the corner leading a horse not as tall as Zephyr but in its own way just as beautiful. Immediately she understood why its name was Sauvignon. Its coat was a shiny, coppery red with a stark white mane, tail and diamond-shaped spot just above its nose. Marissa seemed to know the horse at once. And she felt no fear.

As with Zephyr, Donovan kept up a running monologue (or was it a dialogue?) with Sauvignon in Spanish, and the horse waited patiently while Donovan placed a brightly colored blanket over its swayed back, followed by gripping what she'd later learn was the stirrup and cinch in his hand before lifting the saddle over the horse's back and lightly placing it on the blanket. In the interim Diego had come from the barn with a red stair step, its once bright shade adorned with childishly painted flowers now faded and worn. Once Donovan was finished, he swung up on the horse as if it was something he did every day instead of only when his busy schedule allowed. He directed Diego to place the step near the horse.

"Come on, cowgirl," he teased. "You're going to ride behind me."

Diego motioned her over. His smile, and the way Donovan's solid body sat astride the horse, along with the thought that very soon she'd actually have a reason to hold on to him for dear life, propelled her forward. "Sauvignon, this is Marissa," he cooed in the horse's ear, while rubbing its thick, white mane. Diego did the same, in Spanish, and Marissa found herself murmuring *"hola"* as the horse stared wide-eyed and curious at the stranger approaching.

"Are you sure this can hold me?" she asked, looking pointedly at the stair step that had seen better days.

"You and me together," Donovan assured her. "It's

held every Drake kid, cousin and childhood friend for almost three generations. Those flowers you see are Diamond's handiwork from when she fancied herself an artist."

Diego helped her onto the horse's broad back and behind Donovan's equally expansive one. "Put your arms around me and hold on," Donovan said in a way that caused Marissa's triangle to tingle. She put her arms around him. "Tighter," he commanded, and in Marissa's mind he was issuing that command from another place. "Hold on to me and don't let go," he said, his tone low and warm, nodding at Diego as they left the corral and entered the open prairie. "I've got you."

He began with a trot, continually reassuring Marissa that nothing would hurt them. Other times the ride was silent as both of them took in the beauty of the day and the beauty of their bodies' proximity. "I'm going to let her have her head," he finally announced over his shoulder.

"What's that mean?"

"Hang on tight, baby, and find out! Giddyap!"

Marissa let out a squeal as the horse broke into a full gallop. She squeezed her eyes shut and clutched her thighs tightly against Donovan's legs. Soon, however, a thrill rose inside her and she opened her eyes to see the land blurring around her. She could barely believe this was actually her life right now…that she was on a horse and she was having such fun! She whooped with delight, surprising herself.

Donovan laughed, enjoying her newfound pleasure. "Oh, so you're liking this now?" he yelled into the wind.

"Amazingly, yes!"

"Ha! I knew you had a wild side!" Donovan spurred

the horse on, even as he forced his focus on the strength of the rein and the direction of the horse. Otherwise, he'd get lost in the feel of Marissa's thighs pressing against him, her breasts outlined against his back, her smell all around him. He hardened at the thought of her riding him the way she now rode Sauvignon, free and uninhibited, of them pressed together, skin to skin, of him raw and hard and hot inside her. *Son, you've got to saddle the filly before you can ride her, and you've got to ride her, make sure she fits, before you make her your own.*

Chapter 19

After several moments at this exhilarated pace, Donovan pulled the reins and slowed Sauvignon to a trot. They'd reached a thicket of fruit trees, their limbs hanging heavy with apples, pears, oranges and lemons. Donovan decided to give the horse a rest and, after helping Marissa dismount, he reached into the saddle for the blanket and bottles of water that Diego had packed. They picked fruit and after washing it with the water, sat on the blanket and shared family stories.

"Mmm, this is so good," Marissa said, biting into a juicy red apple. "We only had citrus trees in our backyard. We drank so much lemonade as children that I thought I'd turn into the yellow fruit."

"Ha! That reminds me of the time Dexter and I held a contest to see who could eat the most apples. Needless to say, that didn't end well."

"What happened?"

"You can't guess? Apples are quite fibrous, which means—"

"Whoa! Too much information!"

"So you get the picture, huh?" Donovan's eyes held a mischievous glint.

"Unfortunately."

"Not only did we eat a bushel, they weren't quite ripe. We spent the night exploding from both ends."

"Ooh, Donovan, that is just nasty!" Marissa swatted at him. Donovan ducked. "Shut! Up!" She tried to maintain the frown but laughed so hard she doubled over. "Did you guys get in trouble?" she asked once she'd caught her breath.

"Didn't you hear what I just said? The night we went through was punishment enough!"

After wiping her eyes, she finished the apple. Spurts of laughter accompanied every bite. "You know I'm never going to look at one of these the same."

"Yes, well, neither have I."

Marissa reached for the bottle of water beside her and leaned back on her elbow. "It sounds like you guys had so much fun growing up."

Donovan nodded. "We did."

"Yours is a wonderful family."

"Thank you. We're blessed."

"Tell me more about your grandparents, David and Mary. You said she was from New York?"

Donovan nodded, having just taken a big bite from the juicy apple, and wriggled his brows at Marissa as he wiped juice off his chin. "Harlem girl, born and bred. My grandfather had gone east to attend Howard University. On his first free weekend, which was his first weekend in D.C., he and some friends caught a train to New York."

"That had to be pretty exciting for a man who'd been born and raised in this part of the world."

"Grandpa always had aspirations," Donovan explained. "Always had what Papa Dee calls the wanderlust to see places and do things. He'd gone south dozens of times but up until then, his seventeenth birthday, he'd never been farther east than Louisiana. He'd always had a fondness for New York though, ever since he was a boy and heard about things like the Harlem Renaissance with all of its prolific poets and writers, artists and activists. But what really drew him there was the music."

"Like who?"

"Ah, man," Donovan said, smiling as he recalled childhoods spent at Grandpa David and Grandma Mary's house, listening to their "old" music and laughing at what looked to Donovan's childhood eyes like outlandish dances. He probably wouldn't have laughed so hard had he known there was a "running man" or a "cabbage patch" in his future. "Jazz greats like Duke Ellington, Cab Calloway, Billie Holiday, Dizzy Gillespie…"

"Your grandfather saw Billie Holiday perform live?"

"That was his and my grandmother's first date."

"Wow." Marissa shook her head in wonder. "All these years married and they met at a club."

"Ha! The more things change the more they stay the same, huh? They tell it best, and it changes depending on the point of view—whether David's or Mary's—but the story goes that Grandpa and three of his buddies walked into Small's Paradise Club and my grandfather sees my grandmother across the room, laughing with some of her friends. He said her smile stopped him in his tracks and he knew in that moment, that instant, that she was going to be his wife. That's what he told his friends."

Marissa's eyes sparkled as she listened. At heart, she was a hopeful romantic albeit one for whom fairy tales were limited to romance novels and movie screens. "What'd they say?"

"What do you think? Laughed at him, dared him to approach her, especially with her looking so chic and urban in her navy blue suit with padded shoulders. It was one of the first times he'd beheld such a fine pair of legs in silky nylons. Grandpa was undeterred. He walked over, hat in hand, and she not only refused him but called him a country bumpkin straight out."

"She didn't! Your Grandma Mary?"

"She did." Donovan was really laughing now. "But little did she know that Grandpa loves a challenge as much as he loves wine. Somehow he finagled her number and on that first date to see Billie Holiday, just a few months after her legendary appearance at Carnegie Hall, he brought along a bottle of Papa Drake's Wines. All of this—" Donovan swept his hand across the land "—was still a vision in Papa Dee's eye back then. It would be another five years before the first large plot of grapes were planted, and another ten before Drake Wines as we know it was born. But after that bottle of wine and the Holiday concert? For David, Jr., and Mary the rest, as they say, is history."

As if on cue, Donovan stood, walked over to the saddle and pulled out his last treat…a bottle of wine. "The timing is coincidental," he said, in answer to the quizzical, slightly worried, slightly wonder-filled look on

Marissa's face. "I'm not forgetting what you said about this being a professional relationship. Fortunately for us, drinking wine is a job requirement." He produced a small corkscrew and two plastic cups and, after opening the bottle, walked back over to where Marissa sat on the blanket.

He held up his cup. "To a great assistant, whose help this week has been invaluable."

"To your family, especially the elders," Marissa replied, her tone more serious than Donovan's light-hearted delivery. "Whose vision made this day and this moment."

And, just like that, the moment shifted. Her words produced an awareness of who they were and where they were and what they both felt but continued to try and deny. Donovan's eyes darkened as he drank in her countenance, the lips that she licked when nervous, like now. Her eyes searched his as well, noted how his breathing had increased. She broke the stare, and took a nervous sip of the wine. But Donovan wasn't willing, or able, to let the moment go so quickly. He leaned over, slowly, as if dealing with a skittish mare that might bolt from sudden movement, and placed the lightest of kisses on her forehead.

"That was beautiful," he said, his eyes traveling once more to her lips before looking back at her.

Donovan had her flustered, but Marissa hid it behind taking a keen interest in the wine bottle label, reading it as though later on its contents would be a test question. "Wow. The insides of my legs are throbbing." With cup in hand, she gracefully rose to her knees before standing. It was true, her legs did hurt. But she stood less to get away from the pain in her thighs and more to get away from the burgeoning heat happening between them.

"You'll want to take a hot shower tonight, or a good soak. The rooms are stocked with healing salts. You'll want to use that, along with the tiger balm that is sold in the gift shop."

Marissa declined a second glass of wine. After corking the remainder and cleaning up their mini-picnic area, Donovan hoisted her and then himself back into the saddle. The ride back was mostly quiet, each absorbed in their own thoughts and the beauty of the day. As he enjoyed the earth pounding beneath him and the sky overhead, Donovan did the math. Four days, after today that's all he had left. Because the 4th was the following Friday, and because they weren't working tomorrow, he had just four more days to convince Marissa that he was the one she didn't even know she was waiting for.

Chapter 20

About a mile out, Donovan pulled on the reins and slowed the pace. "Time to cool down, buddy." When they reached the pond, he stopped and let the horse enjoy a nice long drink. Afterward, satisfied that the mare was sufficiently cool, he turned her toward the stables. Once there, Sauvignon came to a stop. *"Trabajo bueno,"* he told her. "Good job."

Marissa sighed against his chest. "That. Was. Wonderful." *And so is this.* Before she could stop herself, she squeezed Donovan's lean waist, hugging him tight and pressing herself close against him. He smelled of wind and grass and…masculine goodness. He felt like strength and honor and truth. She didn't want to let him go. But she knew that she should. He was her temporary boss, after all, and as beautiful as the scenery around her was, it was still an extension of the workplace. Wasn't it? *So why is it that right now I don't give a good gosh darn, I just want to jump this man's bones?* Before losing her last ounce of discipline she quickly (yet reluctantly) pulled her arms from around his waist.

He immediately felt the absence of her touch. "I'll dismount first, and then help you," he told her, lithely swinging his leg in front of him and jumping down. He rubbed Sauvignon's nose; loosened the cinch. He then turned to Marissa with arms upraised. Eyes locked. Hearts clenched. Marissa looked from his arms to the ground. There seemed to be quite a distance between them. "Trust me." He reached up, placed his large hands around her small waist and pulled her toward him. He wasn't expecting her to be so light, to feel so good, to smell so sweet, to fit so perfectly against him. He didn't mean to brush her body with his as he lowered her to the ground. It just happened. Just like he didn't mean to reach up and run a firm, thick finger against her baby-soft cheek, or have his head lower at the exact moment that hers tilted upward. Like the sun that shone or the air that lightly whipped around them, some things just naturally took place. Like the spark that ignited as soon as their lips touched. Both knew that what had just gotten started could not be stopped.

The kiss was many things at once: hot, soft, wet and long overdue. Donovan moved his head from side to side, softly rubbing his cushy lips against Marissa's equally thick ones. Mutual sighs caused their breath to mingle. Their touching lips felt like coming home. His hands moved from her waist, wrapped themselves around her lithe body as he flicked his tongue between her slightly opened mouth. A moan escaped her as she opened to receive him, her tongue hurrying to make its acquaintance with his—dueling, swirling, searching. Of their own accord, her arms wrapped themselves around his neck, her hand pressing him closer, pushing him deeper. All thought had fled—of fear, doubt, propriety—replaced by pure, unchecked desire, raging stronger than the brush fire that had taken out half the back forty of the neighboring farm last year.

Through the haze of passion, Donovan heard a soft, neighing sound. *I know, Sauvignon, time to take off the saddle.* This was followed by a very wet nose nudging the back of his head. *Ha! Good idea, old girl.* Donovan heeded Sauvignon's stellar advice and, with tongues still entwining, began walking Marissa backward toward the stable. They were two employees, temporary though they may be, making out in broad open daylight before God and everybody. His mother rarely visited the stables these days, but it would be just his luck for her to decide to try out the telescope Donald had gifted her with at Christmas.

They entered the barn, a cool respite from the blazing sun. It smelled of hay and sweet feed, horse sweat and leather. The thorough cleaning given just that morning prevented it from smelling of something less desirable. No matter. Donovan and Marissa were only aware of each other: the feel of her silky hair as he bunched it in his fingers, how his muscles rolled beneath her hand. He turned so that she was against the wall and lifted his head to look deep into her eyes before continuing the assault. The kiss changed in intensity the way the horse had changed speeds, quickly going from soft and languid to hard and urgent. Breathing intensified as nipples hardened and a shaft became engorged. He raised his head again, this time to rain kisses on her temples, cheeks and forehead. The absence from her mouth caused his mind to clear. Breathing heavily, he leaned his forehead against hers.

"We can't do this." Donovan worked to control his breathing.

"I know." Marissa willed her heart not to beat out of her chest.

"The work," he whispered.

"My crazy friend," she replied in kind.

"Just too complicated."

"Doesn't make sense." She stared into eyes, which mirrored her own, filled to the brim with longing and black with desire.

Breathing slowed.

Time stood still.

"Just one more kiss?"

"Okay."

He thrust his tongue into her mouth. It was as if a starter gun fired, as though lightning flashed through every fiber of her being. Just like that, she was on fire, a tigress raging out of control. Marissa could think of only one possibility to stoke this flame. Mindlessly, she reached for the cotton shirt tucked inside his jeans and pulled it free. But there was still a problem. Too much fabric between them. With not one thought of embarrassment or consequences, she stepped back, pulled her cotton top over her head, threw it to the ground and then fell once again into Donovan's waiting arms. *Ah, better.*

Hard abs. Soft breasts. Donovan agreed. A perfect combination.

Pulling them farther into the barn, Donovan spotted a blanket folded on top of a bale of hay. Later, he'd wonder if Diego had known something before he did, but now he just thanked the gods for its convenience. He disengaged from Marissa just long enough to grab it and spread it on a bed of scattered hay. Dropping to his knees, he paused, looked up and took a moment to drink in the vision before him. She looked like a vineyard nymph, her hair deliciously tousled, her lips wet and swollen from his relentless kisses, smooth chocolate mounds peeking from a lacy, white bra. His eyes traveled down to a smooth, flat stomach. He kissed her inward navel, whipped his tongue inside the belly button indention even as his hands sought and found their target: the jean's zipper.

He undid the button above it, all the while looking into Marissa's eyes. "Are you sure?" She nodded. He smiled, unzipped the pants and pulled them down around curvy hips, thick thighs and strong, sexy calves. His eyes darkened even further as he leaned into her, inhaled the sweetness of her paradise, rubbed his neat goatee against her lacy wisp of a thong. Licking the sides of the triangle of fabric, he caught hints of the unshaven honeypot hidden behind it. His dick hardened further, pushing up against his jeans in a way that was almost unbearable.

Fortunately a rescue was at hand. "Here," Marissa said, kneeling down on the blanket while avoiding his eyes. "Let me." Her movements were not as smooth as Donovan's had been, with slightly shaking fingers working to unclasp the silver buckle, unbutton the fastener and undo the zipper or, rather, unleash the beast. That's what she thought of his manhood: a long, thick bulge against stark white cotton boxers that caused her eyes to widen and her throat to go dry. She'd read about such massive appendages in erotic romances, had even seen one during her one and only experience watching a porno flick. But to see one live, throbbing, in the flesh? It made her heart race even as it made her wet.

"Come here." Donovan shifted so that most of the blanket was exposed. "Lie down." He rose as she lay, and he removed his jeans and boxers. His desire bobbed and weaved like a fencer's sword. He noted Marissa's stare and the slight apprehension that shone in her eyes. "I'll try not to hurt you."

She swallowed. "Okay."

He lay next to her and for a moment, mere seconds really, was content to just look in her eyes. But all too soon his need to touch her, feel her beneath him, overcame him. He placed soft kisses on her face, neck and shoulders as his hand sought and found the valley between her thighs. "Um." He kissed her deeply while his fingers explored, teasing her silky folds, running his thick middle finger between them, swallowing her gasp inside his mouth. With one slight pull and a flick of his wrist, the thong came away from Marissa's body, leaving her fully exposed. She felt free and wanton as the wind played against her skin, along with Donovan's fingers and tongue. He plunged a digit inside her, and she opened wide to accommodate him. His thumb teased her nub, and she thrashed against the blanket, the prickling hay against her back creating a textural contrast to the fire below.

"Donovan, please," she panted, the words surprising to her ears. "I need it. I can't wait."

And there it was, that deep, rumbling chuckle that was all too rare, pouring into her ear as he covered her body. He held himself over her, placed his juicy round tip at the entrance of her heat. She squiggled against it, willing her body to open up and accommodate him. But he was as big as a Louisiana slugger and she was as tight as a drum.

"Relax," he whispered, kissing her everywhere his mouth could reach. "Relax, my sweet Marissa."

It took several moments but finally he was inside her. Donovan lay still, delighting in how tightly she sheathed him, luxuriating in how her feminine flower pulsed around his love muscle. Once adjusted, she began moving beneath him—lazy circles, a sure, slow grind. Donovan smiled, appreciative of the fire he'd discovered underneath her conservative demeanor. There wasn't much time left to prove to Marissa what she needed, to melt the ice around this woman's heart. *Sweet, sweet Marissa. My beautiful filly. I guess it's time to show you right now.* So with that thought, and with a deep thrust, the ride began again…for real.

Chapter 21

Donovan shifted lanes on I-15 North, bobbing his head to the sounds of Anthony Hamilton, one of his favorite artists. His mood was happy, ecstatic even, and it had everything to do with one particular woman and one very special afternoon. A classic that used to play on his grandparent's turntable wafted into his head. *Yes, what a difference a day makes.* Based on how Marissa had reacted after the loving was over and the spell had lifted, his battle to win her heart was nowhere near done. It had been the quietest ride ever back to the hotel and once she'd showered and rejoined him in the office, he knew that it had just begun.

"We need to talk about what happened." Marissa entered Donovan's office without knocking: no jewelry, no smile and no preamble.

Donovan nodded. "Have a seat."

"I'd rather not." Realizing that she'd spoken more harshly than intended, and that, literal romp in the hay aside, Donovan was technically still her boss and not so technically her permanent employer's brother-in-law, she backtracked. "What I mean is, there's a lot of work to be done and what I have to say won't take long. So…I'd rather stand."

"Please, Marissa…"

She was glad he couldn't see how her name rolling off his tongue now affected her: a squiggle here, clenched muscles down there, heat pulsating throughout her very core.

He didn't have to. Donovan knew that Marissa had to be upset; that like him she preferred to maintain control. She was probably angry that she'd lost it. Donovan, however, was shaken, not scared. For now he'd go easy…but he had no intention of letting her go. He motioned for her to take a seat in front of him. She reluctantly complied. He sat back in the chair: demeanor relaxed, voice steady and calm. "What happened just now was a moment that neither of us expected. But since the remainder of your time here will require us to work together extremely intensely—"

That's what I'm afraid of.

"and very closely—"

I'm toast.

"I'm hoping that the professional camaraderie we've created will allow us to finish the task in stellar fashion. I'm sure you want me to forget this afternoon. That's not going to happen." He looked at Marissa without blinking. She looked away. "But I will respect what I'm sure are your wishes and conduct myself in a proficient, platonic manner. If that's what you want."

"It's exactly what I want." *So why does it feel so terrible? Because you're a liar, that's why!*

"Fair enough." He looked at his watch. "I have a luncheon meeting in an hour, and I believe that the majority of what else I have to accomplish today can be done online. So this afternoon, if it will make you feel better, you'll have the office all to yourself." A bittersweet smile scampered across his face.

Little did he know it, but Marissa wanted to catch that smile, put in her pocket and save it for when she was back working at Boss Construction and once again sleeping in her San Diego bedroom—alone. Instead she stood, squared her shoulders and, with a thankyou that couldn't have been delivered more curtly than if it had been by a staff sergeant to an underling, she left his office.

Thirty minutes later, Donovan left for the day.

Donovan's cell phone rang, bringing him out of his musings. "Sharon!"

"Wow, somebody's happy. And here I thought you couldn't live without me."

"Ha! Barely. How are you?"

"Much better, thank you. The doctors say I may be able to leave in the next few days. I got the flowers, the candy, the bear and the wine. Of course, they confiscated the latter, but the gesture was appreciated."

"Nothing beats a failure but a try."

"Most wouldn't take you for a bad boy, Donovan Drake. But I know differently. You're incorrigible."

"I knew that Patrice would tell you about it. Hoped that it would put a smile on your face."

"That it did. How are things at the office?"

"As under control as it can be without you around. Diamond's husband's assistant is helping me. She's proficient, a speedy typist, a workaholic—" *amazing lover* "—we're doing okay."

"She sounds wonderful. Do I need to be worried about my job?"

"Never that. You're irreplaceable. Which is why I'm on my way to L.A. to see with my own eyes that the doctors are doing their job."

"Donovan! I told you not to bother."

"And it seems as though I'm coming up just in time, too. Somebody seems to have forgotten who's boss."

Marissa was thinking about bosses, too, and it wasn't Jackson Wright. Until now, she would not have thought it possible to have one single thought consume you for twenty-four hours. Even in sleep, she'd dreamt of him. Donovan. Heard his laugh, smelled his scent, felt him thick and deep inside her. By morning she believed that the dull ache between her legs was not the residue of her ride on Sauvignon but the relished reminder of Donovan riding her. One thing she now knew for sure: with the other two men she'd been with, she'd only had sex. Yesterday, for the very first time, she'd made love. It was the best possible man at the worse possible moment. Or was it? The more she thought about it, the less she was sure.

Traffic was light as Marissa smoothly navigated her silver Honda over three lanes and prepared to exit I-15 South, just north of downtown San Diego and just minutes from her destination: the Blessed Assurance Baptist Church. When she arrived in what had been her home away from home for a large part of her life, the crowd was bustling, the mood was joyful and praise and worship were in full swing. After a procession of waves and hugs from the parking lot to the pew, she settled in to enjoy the service. And she did. So much so that midway through the sermon that dealt with God's favor, man's faith and finding the balance, she was convinced that the minister was speaking directly to her. He admonished the parishioners to shake off the fears of the past and embrace the glorious future that God intended. "You've prayed for a blessing, a miracle," he intoned. "And then when God sends it, you turn and run away!"

She joined the shouts of "Amen, Pastor!" and "Hallelujah!" and by the time service had ended, her decision had changed and her mind had been made up. She was going to come clean with Donovan, take a chance with her feelings. He had assumed that she wanted him to forget what happened between them. He assured her that he wouldn't. Later today, she'd assure him that not only was amnesia not what she wanted, but that she'd like to give him more such moments to be remembered.

Those heady thoughts, that giddy feeling, lasted fifteen whole minutes. That's how long it took for her to navigate the crowd, exit the church, walk down the steps and run almost directly into Steven McCain.

Chapter 22

"Whoa!" Steven turned. When he realized who had bumped him, he broke into a wide smile. "Just what I've always wanted—a beautiful woman running into my arms."

Marissa stepped back, quickly assessing the situation. Steven was with his friend, Antonio, so that helped. Antonio had always seemed like a stand-up guy, low-key, not prone to histrionics. There's no way he'd let Steven act a fool on the Lord's day right in front of His house. *Maybe I can get through this without tears. Or bloodshed.* She lifted her chin, determined to try.

"Hello, Steven, Antonio." When he leaned over, she gave Antonio a quick hug.

"What? No hug for me?"

"Sorry, dude, I'm all out." The cheeriness in her voice was as fake as snow in summer, but it sounded real enough. "I have a handshake though."

Steven took her hand, but when he lifted it to his mouth she pulled away. His eyes narrowed. "Damn, baby girl. If I didn't know better, I'd think you were still trying to block a brother, that you still have attitude about a lie told to you, about a situation that should have been forgiven. Being that we're here at church and all."

"All is forgiven, Steven. But nothing is forgotten. That's the difference. Y'all brothers have a blessed day."

She'd only taken one step before Steven grabbed her arm. "What's the rush, *sister?* Aren't you going to fellowship with your fellow congregants as the pastor suggested?" He smiled, as if to show that what he said was indeed a question and not a demand.

"That's what I just did," Marissa retorted, trying to keep her tone light as well.

"Tony and I were just getting ready to go grab a bite. Care to join us?"

"No, thanks. I already have plans." Once again, she turned to walk away, ready to smack Steven with her purse if he tried to detain her.

He didn't, but he fell into step right beside her. "Hey, Tony," he said, his voice still light and playful. "Marissa doesn't believe that I have pictures of her, the ones I told you about."

Marissa huffed, slowly losing control of the peace the service had just provided. "Steven, please. Why don't you give it a rest?" She turned to Antonio. "Tony, like thousands of teens transitioning into adulthood, I made some decisions that if it were possible I'd take back. One of them is that I posed nude for an art class. It was done very tastefully and—" she whipped around to Steven "—*no* pictures were taken." She stopped and confronted Steven. "There. You satisfied?" She began walking even faster to her car.

"Don't even worry about that, Marissa," Antonio said. "Like the reverend said, the past is the past." He gave a warning look to Steven. "Cut it out, man."

Steven ignored Antonio and continued following Marissa. "No pictures were taken during class, but after class? In that little dressing room where you'd stored your clothes?" Marissa's steps faltered the slightest bit. "Ha! Yeah, you remember. But what you might not have known is that there was a storage room with an opening just large enough to offer a full view of everything happening on the other side of the wall."

Marissa stopped in her tracks. "You're a liar!"

"Ha! You wish."

"A sick pervert. A worthless lowlife. I can't believe that I ever called you friend."

"Tony, man, it's funny what people will do when they think they're by themselves. When they think that no one's watching."

Marissa neared her car. She lifted her arm to disengage the locks, opening the door as soon as she reached it. She'd have closed it, but Steven held it firm.

Antonio took a step forward. "Steven, that's enough! Come on, man—"

"Look, don't involve yourself in what ain't your business. I just want to talk to her." He turned to Marissa, softened his voice. "Five minutes. That's all."

Taking a deep breath, Marissa placed her keys in the ignition and her phone by her side. In case she needed to dial 911. She looked at Antonio and nodded, but was grateful that he didn't walk too far away. "Okay, Steven. Five minutes."

"I want to go out with you."

"Not happening."

"I didn't do what that couple said that I did."

Marissa glared at him. "You didn't spike my drink? You didn't try to assault me with a date rape drug?"

Steven shook his head. "I swear."

"Fine. I believe you." She didn't believe him for a second. "But the fact remains that I don't want to go out with you, Steven. I don't want to date you. And, unfortunately, because I don't trust you, we can't be friends again."

"How is it that you could be a slut and sleep with all those other guys but not me? Huh?"

"That's it. I'm leaving." She started the ignition and tried to close the door. "Let go, Steven!"

"Man, you heard her." Antonio walked up next to Steven and stood firm. "Let her go."

"Before it's over, you're going to be with me. And I'd better not see you with nobody else! Or I'll put those pics on blast so fast, send them out to the world. Starting with Chicago and the congregation at your daddy's new mega-church."

As soon as Steven released the door, Marissa slammed it, put the car in drive and raced from the parking lot. She refused to cry, kept herself composed all the way to her parents' old neighborhood, where she had dinner with friends. Afterward, she returned to her apartment. She'd washed the clothes from last week and picked out outfits for her remaining week at work. All that was left to do before returning to the resort was fold the last load of clothes and pack her bags. Still, no tears. *He's bluffing. There's no way that he saw....* As she set about doing this last chore she tried to push Steven's threat out of her mind. Much, much easier said than done.

The phone rang. *Thank God!* Grateful for the distraction, she hurried to where she'd left her purse in the living room, retrieved her cell and caught the call on the fourth ring. "Hello, Mom!"

"Hello, Marissa. It sounds like you're in good spirits. Did you go to church today?"

Girl, this good mood started yesterday afternoon! Forgetting her angst for a moment, Marissa almost laughed out loud. But she resisted the urge to tell her mom about Donovan. *What could come of what happened in the barn?* Steven's face flashed before her. *Nothing.* "I did, and it was excellent. And then I had lunch with the Johnsons."

"Oh, that's fabulous! How are they?"

Marissa gave her mother a brief update and shared the day's message. "The church was full and the choir was rocking. It was a really good day. How are you doing? How is Dad?"

"We're fine, baby, doing our best to handle the responsibilities of this large congregation. But we're feeling more at home here with each passing day. The members are great. In fact, that's why I'm calling. We've been invited to join one of the families at their home in the country for the Fourth of July. I didn't know if you had plans and wanted you to know that you are welcome to join us in Chicago."

"Thanks, Mom. I'm not sure what I'll be doing, but I'll think about it and check out air fares just in case."

"Don't worry about cost, darling. Dad will give you his credit card number. We'd love to see you. You will be off that weekend, correct? And finished with the project you were working on the last time we talked?"

"Yes, I should be. Jackson and Diamond are due back right after the holiday."

"I'm sure you'll be happy to get back to familiar surroundings."

Truth was, when it came to leaving Drake Resorts in general and Donovan in particular, happy was not the emotion she felt. Not at all.

"Marissa, are you all right? Is there something going on that you'd like to talk about?"

There went Yolanda, turning that mother radar on. She'd always had the ability to sense when things weren't quite well with Marissa, even when she tried rocking the happy face. "Actually, Mom, there is something I'd like to ask you."

"Yes?"

"When you were a teenager, did you ever do anything crazy, something that you could kick yourself for? Something that you'd be absolutely appalled if anyone ever found out?"

"Oh, dear," Yolanda said with a slight chuckle. "Unfortunately, I have. But I'm afraid that if I told you, then I'd then have to—"

"Kill you!" they said simultaneously, echoing one of her father's favorite retorts.

"Honey, we've all done things of which we're not proud. But you know that once you ask forgiveness, then whatever you've done is gone and forgotten, in the past. God doesn't bring it up again, and you shouldn't either."

"But what if it's something that can be brought up, something in writing or…caught on tape?"

Silence on the other end of the phone and then, "Marissa, is there something specific you're asking?"

She couldn't even bring herself to think about it, let alone speak her deepest fear out loud. "I saw Steven at church today. He made a threatening comment...but I don't believe anything he says."

"Lord, is that boy still bothering you? You need to take out a restraining order against him, Marissa. He seemed like a fine young man when you met him and during the times he was at our house. But the more you tell me about his recent behavior, well, the more I wonder if all of his Crayolas are in the box!"

"Mom!"

"I'm serious, honey. I'm growing concerned."

Marissa knew her mom would go ballistic if she knew about their last "date." And her dad would more than likely go to prison for murder. "Don't worry about it, Mom. I hardly see him anymore, and I probably shouldn't have mentioned it."

"I tell you what, Marissa," Yolanda said, her voice filled with the type of assurance that only a mother can transfer. "The next time what he says causes fear to knock on your heart's door? Send faith to answer it. When faith shows up, fear disappears. "

Tears sprang to her eyes unbidden. It was at times like this when she really missed having her family close and really missed her mom. "I'll remember that, Mom. Thanks."

Chapter 23

By the time Monday morning came and Marissa walked into the executive offices of Drake Wines, she'd almost erased the bad feelings gained from her encounter with Steven. That was due in no small part to her mother's words of wisdom and, once she'd arrived back at Drake Wines Resort and Spa, the invitation she'd found for another spa visit under her door. Through a little detective work, she'd found out that those full-service appointments were not cheap. No money came out of Donovan's pocket, but still. The thought was nice, as was the fact that he had to have been thinking about her to have made the reservations in the first place. In spite of Steven's threat, there was a glimmer of hope for a future with Donovan.

This time the treatment took place in the hotel spa. After two hours of delicious pampering, of being wrapped and waxed and flexed and peeled and scrubbed and soothed, Marissa had fairly floated back to her room, ordered a light salad for dinner, watched a movie and, after mentally reliving every single second of her tryst with Donovan, fell into a deep, dreamless sleep. Because of the profound rest, she figured, she'd awakened early, refreshed and ready to go. That's why she sat at her desk at eight-fifteen, having downed a bagel and orange juice, her coffee at the ready, inputting information into the computer as if she were moving to China herself.

"Wow! Good morning!" Marissa startled a bit at the voice, then smiled as she saw Diamond's assistant, Kathleen Fitzpatrick, standing just inside the finance department's doors. "I thought I heard activity back here, but figured it was my cockled brain since I know the guys who get here early." Kat lowered her voice and put her hand to her mouth as if sharing a valuable secret. "It's usually not the guys in this department."

"I heard that, Kat," said a voice from behind her.

Kathleen turned, and Marissa looked up to see Donovan appear at the door, give Kathleen a hug around the shoulder and walk into the room. Carrying flowers.

"Two early birds," Kathleen said, her green eyes twinkling as she eyed the flowers and then the look on Marissa's face. "What hot project is going on in this department?"

"Just back from vacation and I see you're already about to wear out your welcome, Mrs. Fitzpatrick," Donovan said without an ounce of embarrassment or guilt. "But if you must know, these are for Marissa—" he made a show of presenting her with the bouquet "—because of the excellent work she's done so far and for what I'm sure we'll continue to see over these next several days."

"Well, well, don't you rate," Kathleen said with an exaggerated wink at Marissa. "But you'd better get those out of here before Sharon comes back. Lord knows when was the last time you got that woman anything and she's been here since dog was a pup!"

"Kathleen, you know you're wrong," Donovan said between guffaws. "Sharon knows how much she's appreciated. In fact, you'll be happy to know that I personally delivered a bouquet to her just yesterday."

"Really? You saw her?" Kathleen's interest was genuine. She and Sharon were two of the company's longest-running employees. "I meant to call once we got back from vacation, but the grandkids came over and time got away."

"I spent yesterday afternoon with her and her daughter. She put up a valiant and cheery front, but I could tell she's still pretty weak. And she's lost weight."

"I need to get up to L.A. and see her."

"She'll appreciate it. They hope to release her in a couple days, but she'll be at her daughter's house for at least another week. In fact—" Donovan made an exaggerated show of looking at his watch "—unless you have a lot to do, why don't you go right now? After all, it's work related. And it will keep you out of my hair!"

"Fine, I know how to leave when I'm not wanted. Marissa, call me if the warden here lets you out of your cell. If I'm back in time, we'll do lunch. And if not today, tomorrow."

"Ha! Will do, Kat. Thanks." Marissa waited a beat, during which time she inhaled the fragrance from the bouquet of flowers. The only ones she could identify were the lilies, large petals of deep pink with ruby red centers and spots and orange whiskers. "These are very beautiful, Donovan. You really didn't have to, especially considering the gift I found under my door last night."

"Hmm," Donovan asked looking around. "Pray tell, what was that?"

"Yeah, right. I'm sure you have no idea who arranged that. I'll be sure and tell Jackson how well I was treated while I was here. Boss man will have to step up his game when he comes back."

"That conversation should prove interesting."

"Ha! You think?"

Donovan lowered his voice. "Of course, those flowers have nothing to do with your performance at the office."

Marissa felt instant heat, a flush creep from her neck to her chin. And from her navel to her nana. Simultaneously. With eyes darting around, she murmured, "I thought we weren't going to talk about that. Professional, that's our word…right?"

"Right." He stood straight, his hands clasped behind him, his tone clipped and formal, rocking back on his heels. "How was church?"

"Good," Marissa said with a smile that turned to a scowl when she remembered how her Sunday meeting had ended. *Maybe he didn't notice.*

"What kind of good news elicits a frown?"

He did notice. "The message was great and timely." She told him the title. "And then I stepped outside the church and walked right into Satan."

"Let me guess. Steven."

"Can you believe it?"

"What happened?"

"Nothing serious. Just him being his usual irritating self. But I've decided not to let him bother me anymore. I'm finally ready to move on with my life."

That statement hung in the air, dancing with all kinds of questions Marissa was certain Donovan wanted to ask but none she wanted to answer. Before he could ask her anything else, two of the company's accountants showed up. Within fifteen minutes the office was in full swing.

Because of last week's meetings with the Asian consortium, Donovan's calendar was doubly busy this week: meetings with management, overseeing sales and other general tending of the company operations. After he left her desk, she only saw Donovan once all morning. After a refreshing and informative lunch with Kathleen, she didn't see him at all until just before it was time for her to leave the office.

He entered her area just as she turned off her computer. "What? The workaholic is actually leaving at five?"

"It's been a very productive day. Kat is now helping input data so we're flying through those pages."

"A good woman, that Kathleen Fitzpatrick. And the world's best busybody. What did she tell you about me?"

"You?" Marissa's look was as innocent as a newborn babe's. "Why, Mr. Drake, we didn't mention you at all!"

"Ha! You may not have said my name but I guarantee you Kat did."

"What she shared was all good, promise."

"Then you'll have no problem *sharing* with me. Come on, let's have dinner."

Marissa waited until an accountant walked past

them. Lowering her voice, she murmured, "I'm not sure that's a good idea."

Donovan's eyes lowered to her lips. "It's not the only idea, trust me. Just the first one."

She had to ask. "And the second?"

"Checking out Chardonnay, and I *don't* mean our latest vintage."

He meant her suite. *Dayum!* She admired brother man's skills, in spite of herself. "I thought you said we weren't going to do this."

"I hadn't counted on not being able to live without you."

"That we were going to remain professional." Lowering her already low voice to a whisper, she hissed, "Platonic."

His shrug was devil-may-care, his smile sexy. "It's simple, girl. I lied."

"What if someone sees us?" Marissa reached for her purse; her actions conveying she didn't care if they did. "What if we get caught?"

"I've got connections with management. We won't write you up."

And just like that, the two reconnected. Dinner and then…round two.

Chapter 24

Morning, my sweet Marissa: I'll be out of the office for most of the day. Have dinner with me. D.

This was the text that greeted Marissa as she woke up bright and early for her last day temping for Donovan Drake. The last few days had been a whirlwind of work, eat, love, work, eat, love, over and again. Because of Kat's help, the bulk of the project was finished; today would be tying up loose ends and having a major powwow with her so that when Sharon returned to work Kat could easily bring her up to speed. Marissa read the text again, and a third time, her stomach roiling with a slew of emotions. She was in like, in lust, ecstatic, afraid. Nothing had gone the way she'd planned, but everything had turned out better than she'd hoped. Deciding to live in the moment, she'd simply followed

Donovan's lead, did what he told her, met when he summoned, loved him when he appeared. *But what now?* They hadn't discussed the future, hadn't talked about life post work assignment. Was this a "last supper" invite, a fond farewell, a bon voyage, a thanks for the memories before goodbye?

There was only one way to find out. Marissa's response was short and sweet. Yes. After showering, she checked her phone.

Great! My place. D.

He'd texted his address. An invite to his home. That meant something, didn't it? But what? Tired of thinking, she donned an oversize top, a pair of jeans and sandals, then reached for the bags that she'd packed last night and was out the door. No matter what happened tomorrow, today she checked out of paradise.

The rest of the day passed in a blur of final entries and goodbyes; even Donovan's crazy brother Dexter stopped by her desk and paid her a visit.

"I see you survived The Don."

"His bark was worse than his bite, I guess." Then thinking of the way he'd used his teeth last evening, Marissa almost blushed. She hurried on, lest Dexter notice her discomfort. "Kathleen's returning was a huge help. She knows her way around a computer. With her here, really, it's been a breeze."

"So, what now? You mosey on back to Boss Construction without looking back?" The gleam in Dexter's eye suggested his question had nothing to do with administrative assistance.

Has he seen us? Does he know? Did Donovan tell

him? If not, considering the tightness of the Drake clan, it was only a matter of time. "Pretty much. Boss bid on a riverfront project in Louisiana. The decision should come shortly. If we win it, for the next couple months, I'll be up to my ears in work."

Dexter crossed his arms, his look contemplative. "Something tells me we haven't seen the last of you around here. Donovan hasn't invited you to our Fourth of July party?"

"No." *And why not?*

Fortunately, one of the other assistants had come up and interrupted the conversation, Marissa had gone in to meet with Kat and before she knew it five o'clock arrived. Now she was freshly showered and changed, having returned back home, unpacked her bags and rifled through mostly junk mail. Donovan lived close by, about fifteen minutes from her complex. It had been less than twenty-four hours and still she couldn't wait to see him.

In La Jolla, Donovan stirred and then tasted the sauce. Satisfied that it was exactly how he wanted, he readied the bread to be placed into the oven, then removed his apron and walked into the living room. Looking around, he tried to imagine his abode through Marissa's eyes. It was his dream home, but would she like it? They'd been intimate several times, but Donovan felt as though this was a first date. "It is in a way," he admitted to the empty room. After tonight, Donovan planned to invite her to the picnic, introduce her as his woman. He couldn't have been happier that he and Marissa had gotten together, that their love had blossomed. It was time to come out of hiding and take this situation public. He remembered something he'd left in his bedroom and just as he'd retrieved it, the doorbell rang.

He walked to the door, a big smile gracing his face as he opened it. "Hey, you."

With the intimacies they'd shared, it was ridiculous to be shy. But she was. "Hey, yourself."

For several seconds, they simply looked at each other. Donovan finally pulled her to him. "Get in here."

He wrapped his arms around her, kissed her slowly, thoroughly. He loved her lips, couldn't get enough of their sweetness. Sliding his hands from her waist to her butt, he cupped her cheeks and gave a little squeeze. This was undoubtedly one of her best assets. He couldn't get enough of it either. "How'd it go today?"

"Great! Everything was almost done, as you know, so it was mostly about making sure Kat had all of the information to pass on to Sharon. Kat said she was home?"

"At her daughter's house, but doing very well. Thanks for asking about her." He brushed a tendril of hair away from her face, tweaked her cheek. "You don't even know her, but you care. You're a good woman, you know that?"

"It doesn't hurt to be told." She smiled, believing that she could get lost in his eyes. His countenance was unreadable as he continued to stroke her face, and then he ran a hand along her arm, down her back. The moment was ripe with a certain awareness…and something else. *Donovan trying to find a nice way to end this, perhaps?* The very thought almost produced tears. "Nice place," she said a bit too brightly, just to break the mood.

"You like?"

"Very much. Did you have it professionally decorated?"

"Sure did. You know the designer. Her name is Diamond."

"Of course, who else?" Marissa did a 360 degree turn, taking in the living, dining and den areas of the open space, seeing the state-of-the-art kitchen just beyond it. "Very classy. I love her style."

"I'll be happy to give you the personal tour. But for now? Dinner awaits."

"Oh, that reminds me." Marissa held up a wine bag. "It's what I could grab on short notice. I hope you like it."

He reached into the bag and pulled out a bottle of Drake Wines petite sirah, 2007. It was a limited bottling and cost fifty dollars a pop. "You know I'm going to have to reimburse you," he said with feigned chagrin. "But thank you." He kissed her. "This is a very good year." They walked into the dining room, hand in hand.

"How can I help?" Marissa asked.

Donovan opened a drawer on the dining room buffet and pulled out a corkscrew and aerator. He handed them to Marissa. "You can do the honors," he said with a nod toward the bottle.

"What's this?" she asked, holding the glass cylinder up toward the modern, funky chandelier.

"An aerator." Donovan reached for the wine bottle and then for the opener. When she handed him the corkscrew, their fingers touched. Sparks flew. "Stop shocking me, woman!"

"I was just getting ready to demand the same thing!"

"What can I say? I'll always turn you on."

Marissa groaned. "That was *really* corny."

"Yeah, but it made you smile." After explaining the simple device that helped wine breathe instantly, he poured the fruity concoction through the opening. The whirring sound filled the silence as he filled their glasses. Once done, he handed her a glass. "You first."

"Me?" Marissa thought for a moment. "To a relentless slave driver."

"What?"

"Okay," Marissa said with a chuckle. "To a job well done? How's that?"

"About average," Donovan said in the straightforward manner Marissa both loved and abhorred. "How about…to new beginnings, to us." He paused and placed a whispery kiss on her parted lips. "And to the first night spent with you where I don't have to creep before morning!"

"Ha! Hear, hear!" They drank. "Donovan, you don't have to—"

"Oh, here you go, getting ready to mess with the mood. Dinner's almost ready. Make yourself at home. We'll eat first. And talk later. Deal?"

"Deal."

Chapter 25

"This is delicious," Marissa said after taking her first bite of Donovan's spaghetti. "What restaurant is this from?"

"Uh, that would be my kitchen?"

"You did this?"

"You doubt it?"

"Wow, you really can cook!"

"Girl, I told you."

It was a beautiful evening, and after Marissa raved about it, they had decided to dine at the table on Donovan's back patio, which had been designed as an outdoor living space.

"Who taught you to cook?" She bit into a piece of heavily buttered Texas toast, the perfect complement to the herb salad dotted with shaved Parmesan. "Your mom?"

"Grandma Mary," Donovan replied. "Her thinking was a man who knew how to cook would never go hungry. So she made sure all of us could do well enough to get by."

"So all of the Drake men cook, even Dexter?"

"Dexter's skills are probably rusty," Donovan admitted. "But even he learned how to back in the day. Our cousins, the Drakes of Louisiana? They can really throw down—gumbo, jambalaya, crawfish bisque."

"Crawfish? What's that?"

"Ah, girl. 'Good eating,' is what Papa Dee would say. They're kind of like lobsters," he offered at last, "but chewier, and smaller, too. You've never been to Louisiana?" Marissa shook her head. "Not even New Orleans?"

"No. I've always wanted to go though."

"I'll take you."

Marissa thought of a memory from Diamond's wedding and couldn't help but laugh.

"What?"

"Your cousin, Reginald, has beat you to the punch. He said on my first visit, he had to be my tour guide."

"Yeah, whatever. He'll be squiring two of us around town." In fashion typical of The Don, he virtually inhaled half of the food on his plate within minutes, stopping long enough to wipe his mouth and have a sip of wine. "So…tell me about life in the home of a minister? I honestly can't imagine it."

Marissa reached for her wineglass and took a slow sip as she considered the question. "Fairly normal, really, but then again, I have nothing else to compare. My daddy was called to preach—" she made air quotes "—when I was around ten years old. Ours was always a religious household so nothing changed for me." She shrugged.

"Religious household? What does that mean? You guys pray ten times a day, say Hail Marys, what?"

Marissa laughed. "Geez, you aren't familiar, are you?"

Donovan shook his head. "Papa Dee always said half the sinners would probably end up singing in heaven's choir while half the pious Sunday bench warmers would probably split hell wide open."

"Ha! Your Papa Dee's a hoot, but he may have a point. To your question, hailing Mary is part of the Catholic ritual, and, no, praying ten times a day isn't required. There was always prayer at dinner and church on Sundays and Wednesday," Marissa continued, counting on her fingers. "Tuesday night was choir rehearsal, Friday night was sick and shut-in prayer. If there was a youth function, that happened on Saturday."

Donovan's look was deadpan. "You're kidding, right?"

"No. When I say that Blessed Assurance was my second home, I really, really mean it."

"So why'd your parents leave?"

"Dad got an offer that he couldn't refuse, heading up a church with over five thousand members. There's international connections, a TV ministry—"

"I can see your dad on that religious channel, hooting and hollering like…what's his name?"

"No to whoever it is you may have seen or be thinking about. My dad is more a teacher than a preacher. But yes, he's on television weekly and is seen around the world."

"So in church circles, you're almost like a celebrity."

"My dad is, and, yes, people know my name. Some-times popularity is highly overrated, especially when…"

"When what?"

"Never mind. Could you pass me the basket of bread?"

He did, and though he felt she wanted to change the subject, he was genuinely intrigued. "Did your parents expect you to be perfect?"

"Not exactly. But my brother and I were always aware of our last name. There's a general belief that ministers' children are wild, but that isn't always so. Even without the prodding, I was a pretty good kid."

"You never wanted to lash out against the establish-ment, never tried to rebel?"

"Sure, I did. Let's see, there was the time I was twelve and wanted to wear makeup to the movies. My father said no. I promptly disobeyed him and after putting my face on at my friend's house, ran into my mother at the mall."

"What happened?"

"She had mercy, didn't tell my father. I went into the bathroom, washed it off and wore a fresh-face sulk for the rest of the night. Then there were the rap CDs I had to hide and the toe ring I'd slip on when out of parental radar range. But I wasn't a drinker, never did drugs. Aside from a crazy stunt I pulled in college, it was all pretty tame."

"What happened in college?"

"Something I wish had not occurred."

This time, thankfully, Donovan let the subject pass. They continued to converse and, once dinner was over, took the dishes back into the house and put away the foodstuffs. "Leave the dishes," Donovan said when Marissa asked about a dishwasher. "My housekeeper does them."

"Dinner was wonderful, Donovan. And so is your home."

"Are you ready for the rest of the tour?"

"Of course!"

They navigated past the open living space to the upstairs, where he pointed out each of the three bedrooms, including a to-die-for master suite, the three and a half baths and the great room before returning downstairs to Donovan's favorite spot in the house. It was the room that was next to the patio. A man cave to be sure, but classy, dominated in the center by a custom-made pool table.

"This is nice," she said.

"You shoot?"

"I do all right."

"Uh-oh. Those sound like fighting words. Do you want to play?"

"Do you want to lose?"

"Ha! Listen to you. Rack 'em up, shorty."

They began playing a friendly game of eight ball— Marissa, solids and Donovan, stripes. He'd broken and sank one ball when he did so. He made the next few shots before it was Marissa's turn. When her time came up, she took a long moment to scrutinize the table, checking her options, chalking her cue. She decided to go for the corner pocket and leaned over, holding the cue stick the way her brother had taught her all those years ago. She was so focused on hitting the ball that she was totally unaware of the pair of chocolate eyes that were focused on her.

They continued playing around the table until only

two balls were left: the five ball, which belonged to Marissa, and the eight ball, which Donovan needed to sink to win. Only problem was, her ball was between the cue ball and the eight ball.

"Looks like somebody is in trouble," Marissa taunted as she looked at Donovan's impossible situation on the pool table.

"Looks can be deceiving," Donovan replied, cool as a breeze.

"The way I see it you have two options, either scratch or sink my ball. Either way, I win."

"And the way I see it," Donovan said, aiming his cue stick in a way that seemed to point directly at Marissa's ball, giving her the win, "I have three." He struck the cue ball with such force that it bounced off the table, jumped over Marissa's ball, rolled into the eight ball and pushed it right into the pocket.

"Wait! That was a trick shot!" Marissa said with a stamp of the foot.

"A bit competitive, are we?"

"Seriously, how'd you do that?"

"Come here," Donovan said with a laugh. "I'll show you."

She walked over to where he stood. He retrieved the ball and then came up behind her, so that he could guide her hands as she held the stick. "Okay, aim the stick at the bottom of the cue ball, like this." He guided her arm, being careful not to touch her with the rest of his body, so that it tapped the cue ball at just the right spot, a low spot at the center of the ball. "Feel it? Feel how I'm guiding you and where the cue is supposed to go?"

"I feel something all right," Marissa said, her voice sultry, her eyes glazed as she turned in his arms.

"Um," Donovan nuzzled against her neck. "Now look who's playing dirty."

She reached around, cupped his behind. That in four days she'd gone from celibate conservative to an insatiable sex kitten wasn't lost on her. The transition felt good. So rather than think about it, she rolled with it. "Do you have a problem with the moves I'm making?"

"Not at all, my sweet Marissa. I'm getting ready to make one myself."

Taking her hand, Donovan led them to the master suite she'd seen minutes ago—the one with ebony wood floors, gray silk walls and navy accents; with the king-size poster bed covered with a custom-made flannel cover. From the game room to the bedroom he held her hand, slowly stroking her palm with his thumb in slow, lazy circles as his tongue had done.

They reached the bed. He turned to face her, drank in her beauty, swept an errant curl behind her ear. "I'm so happy you're here, in *my* home, getting ready to climb into *my* bed."

"Me, too. I wasn't sure if—"

"Shh, I know. Me, either. We'll deal with that later. Tomorrow."

Resting his forehead against hers, he reached for the ribbon at the top of her sundress, the one he'd eyed all evening, all dainty and feminine near the curves of her breasts. He pulled and it came undone, exposing the top of her globe. He kissed her there. Once. Again.

"Is this okay?" he asked.

"You know it is."

"Yes, I know." He was being the gentleman that he'd promised he would that first time they'd come together following the romp in the hay. On her back and shoulders there'd been scratch marks. He'd felt badly and told her so. Saying that she hadn't felt a thing hadn't mattered. He'd neglected taking care of his baby and for him that was *so* not okay.

Marissa reached for the hem of her dress and pulled it over her head. She stood there, bare, beautiful, in a lacy cream bra and matching thong that emitted a singular message: *snatch me off.* But he didn't. He took his time because there would be no running off in the morning. Placing his large hands on the lacy cups and squeezing gently, he peered deep into Marissa's eyes. They kissed again, and it was as if they breathed each other's air, so deep were they in the exploration of the other's being, so much did they want to both give and receive. Finally, he couldn't stand it anymore. He noticed the front clasp on the bra and placed his finger on it.

"May I?" he asked.

"You know that you can," was Marissa's breathless reply.

He unsnapped her, and her girls swayed their hallelujah. His mouth watered, and he closed his eyes against the rush of desire. *Slow your roll, Don. Take your time. All night, remember?* He reached up and tweaked one nipple and then the other. "Have I told you lately that you're beautiful?"

"Thank you."

He placed his mouth where his fingers had been. "You taste good, too."

Had Marissa been able to remember words at this moment, she would have thanked him again for the compliment. Donovan stepped away, and she instantly missed his touch. His eyes never left hers as he pulled the casual shirt he wore over his head, undid the clasp to his khaki shorts and let them fall to the floor, revealing black boxers and the massive instrument that she'd come to know and love straining the light material. She reached for it, gently outlined it through the fabric before reaching inside and boldly taking hold.

Donovan hissed and stayed her hand. "I want this to be all about you tonight."

"No way," she quickly countered. "This is going to be an equal opportunity evening."

"Then at the very least, may I say ladies first?"

Her chuckle was decadent. "You may."

He guided them to the bed. They lay down and for a while, he just hugged her. His heart beat a fast and erratic rhythm that matched Marissa's. And then he began to kiss her, slowly, starting at the temple nearest his lips and then her ear, over to her eyelid, down to her nose and over to her cheek. Finally finding her mouth, he claimed it in a passionate fashion, thrusting his tongue inside her warmth before pulling back and gently biting her lower lip. And the kisses continued, down her neck, over to her shoulder, licking her flesh and relishing the saltiness of her skin. All the while he played lightly with her nipples, teasing them until they stood at attention, begging to be sucked.

He obliged. Marissa squirmed, lost in a haze of desire that only Donovan could create. While he navigated her body like a GPS system, he never took the same journey twice. This time, after taking his tongue on a meandering journey from one nipple to the other, down to her stomach and tickling her navel, he shifted his body and continued the journey south. He trailed a flurry of kisses along her thigh, lightly massaging her legs along the way, his teeth skimming her calves and ankles. Gently spreading her legs, he reversed course. Marissa grabbed fistfuls of comforter, steeling herself against what was sure to be a lethal assault.

It was.

But not in the way she'd expected. His was a soft, delicate approach; handling her body like fine china, her skin like rare silk. He kissed his way to the inside of her thighs and then oh…so…slowly licked the triangle of fabric between them. "I'd like to remove these—" he ran a finger along the fabric's edge "—and kiss you." He did, right above the panty line, before placing his hand where his tongue had been. "Here."

Marissa swallowed.

"Would you like that?"

She nodded.

He bowed his head. She closed her eyes. And felt his tongue lapping at her already slick folds, bidding her to open wide so that he could reach his target. Again, Marissa wondered about the wanton woman who spread her legs so freely and wondered where the woman who could take or leave sex had gone. He pierced her in two, flicking his tongue against her nub and then, without warning, plunged his strong tongue inside her, once and again. Marissa's breathing increased as she murmured unintelligible sounds. She grabbed his head, silently encouraging him, letting him know that what he was doing was what she was wanting. After what seemed an eternity, he moved over the fabric, flicked her nub with his tongue and that was it. She exploded; seismically, completely—the way she had in the barn that first time, the way that had only happened with Donovan. And all Marissa knew, as she felt herself outside of her body, saw stars and galaxies before floating back down to earth, is that she wanted what had just happened to happen again. And again. And again.

Chapter 26

Marissa awoke to the sound of birds chirping, and when she opened her eyes, it was to the deep, intense orbs of Donovan staring at her. "Good morning."

"Good morning," she said, pulling the sheet to her chin, a move one could consider comical considering how acquainted Donovan had become with her body last night.

"Does it bother you?" he asked softly, running a finger along the side of her arm. "Me looking at you like this?"

Marissa shrugged. "A little."

"Well get used to it, woman," he softly commanded. "Because I intend to be looking at you for a long, long time."

Marissa swallowed what would have been her attempt at a smart retort. Truth of the matter was, she was so delighted by what she'd just heard that no response was needed.

Donovan continued to run his finger along her arm, then her shoulders and neck and along the side of her face. He leaned over and kissed her shoulder, her cheek and temple. Marissa closed her eyes and enjoyed the tender ministrations.

"You know what?" he asked.

"Hmm?"

"I'm sure glad you don't work for me anymore!"

"Ha! Me, too." She turned to face him. "I was so worried that it was over—that this was just a fling."

"I know. Life has thrown you a couple curveballs—translated, knuckleheads—that have shaken your confidence. I can understand that. I've been hurt, too. But I'm not them, baby. I'm for real, with no hidden agenda, no ulterior motive. I just want to be with you. That's all."

He ran his hand along the curve of her back, over the delicious mound of ass that he'd celebrated last night and along her crevice so he could squeeze juicy cheeks. He swore her body could have rivaled the hills and valleys of their property, the slopes and peaks, the beauty of it all. And won hands down. They enjoyed a leisurely kiss before Donovan continued, "So did you think about what I asked last night?"

"Which question?"

Donovan's chuckle was low and sexy. He knew which other questions she was talking about. *Can I kiss you? What about here? Can I go deeper? Am I hurting you, baby?* "No, not those. The one about joining me and my family for the holiday celebration."

"I don't know," Marissa said, sighing as she rolled off of him, but only so that she could begin running her hand over his rock-hard abs and down to his rock-hard manhood. She thrilled at how it grew in her hands, made her feel powerful and wanton, wicked and womanly. "How will your family feel with your bringing over someone you just finished working with?"

"They'd make the correct deduction that you are the one with whom I am now sleeping."

"What? No!"

"Baby, if you're going to be with me than you're going to have to get used to a few things, including our close-knit family having very few secrets from each other. Daddy will be humored and Mama will be thrilled. She's liked you from the jump, since meeting you at the engagement party."

"So you've already talked to them about me?"

"More like the other way around. But I've brought you up a time or two."

"And said what?"

"And that's the second thing you'll have to get used to, every question put to a Drake man doesn't necessarily get answered."

Marissa swatted his chest playfully before resting her head on it. She didn't press. For right now, it was enough that they were together, that she was happy, that she now really knew what it meant to make love. Last night's memories caused her to clench her thighs. She winced, the results of their spirited, sustained lovemaking.

"Are you okay?"

"Just a little sore."

"I'm sorry, baby," he said, kissing her temple. "You'll get used to me in time."

"How do you figure?"

"The more our bodies get acquainted, the easier that sugar box you have down there will let me in."

"Sugar box? Is that a Southern saying?"

"That's Papa Dee talking," Donovan said with a chuckle. "No telling where he got it. He may have even made it up."

Marissa turned to face him. "So you're saying that practice will make perfect, your body to mine?" Donovan nodded. "Then, can we practice some more?"

"Right now?"

"We probably shouldn't, huh? With your family waiting and all."

Donovan began conversing with his body instead of words. He figured he could show her better than he could tell her and if they were late to the picnic, his family would understand.

Three hours later, Donovan and Marissa made their relationship official by showing up hand in hand at the Drakes' party. Genevieve was the first to spot them, and she made a beeline over to where they'd parked.

"Donovan!" She hugged her son and then turned to Marissa. "I'm so glad to see you." They hugged. "Dexter said he'd wanted to invite you, but I assured him that that hadn't been necessary, that there was no way this one here—" she cocked her head toward Donovan "—was letting you go."

"Welcome to the world according to Genevieve," Donovan said dryly. "Has Dad broken the seal on anything yet? Because this is going to be a strong liquor holiday, I can already tell."

"Over by the grills, darling," she replied, entwining her arm with Marissa's. "You don't mind if I steal Marissa for a while, do you? With Diamond away, I've been feeling outnumbered. I'd like to introduce her to Mama and Daddy, and then show her around the estate."

"You might need rescuing," he said to Marissa with a kiss on the cheek. "I've got my phone on me. Call me if you need me."

Marissa chuckled. "Will do." Genevieve's down-home sophistication reminded her of Yolanda. She already liked her immensely.

And with that, Marissa was whisked away. They started inside the estate, where David and Mary Drake were poring over a large jigsaw puzzle, barely begun. "A family tradition," Genevieve explained, after introductions had ended. "Everyone who passes by this room will try and add a piece. By the end of the night, it will be all put together."

After a tour of the house, the short version, they went back outside and over to three temperature-controlled tents that had been set up between the estate and Papa Dee's Suite. Food stations were set up in each; between them, a floor had been erected for dancing. A long row of grills anchored the north side, all different shapes and sizes. "For the barbeque cook-off," Genevieve explained. "The Drake men excuse themselves or else we'd win every year!"

Before the day was over, more than two hundred people, mostly residents from in and around Temecula, passed through the gates of Drake Wines Resort and Spa. Case after case of rich wine flowed, washing down ribs, chicken, seafood, pork and more side dishes than Marissa could have imagined. She'd arrived at the party feeling like Donovan's new woman. She now felt like family.

* * *

"Oh, my goodness," Marissa exclaimed as she and Donovan walked back into his house that evening. "Your family is crazy! That was so much fun!"

"It was pretty fun, wasn't it? Until Papa Dee almost set himself on fire, demanding to hold a Roman candle like a sparkler. That man is a trip."

"I appreciated what he said though. That a man who lived a century could do what he darn well pleased."

"What about a man who's only lived three decades?" Donovan asked, coming behind Marissa and wrapping his arms around her. "Can I do what I please, as well?"

"Depends," she said, following his romantic lead and immediately turning around. It was like they couldn't get enough of each other. After a day filled with furtive glances and suggestive innuendos whispered in each other's ears, Marissa had a feeling this would be another long night. "What do you have in mind?"

"It starts with getting you out of these clothes," Donovan said, even as he easily hoisted her up into his arms and began walking toward the staircase. "And into some water."

"Sounds good so far," Marissa cooed. She'd never been the bold, sensuous woman stating what she wanted and demanding her pleasure. That was a side Donovan had brought out, and one she could get used to. "Then what?"

They'd reached the top of the stairs. Donovan put Marissa down, then led them into the master suite and through to the en suite bath. "Then," he said, unzipping her sundress before raising it over her head, taking a moment to kiss her blackberries masquerading as nipples into hardness and squeezing her booty, "I'm going to give you yet another bath…with my tongue."

Further words ended as a kiss began, slow and languid, first with lips only touching in passing as their heads moved back and forth. Then Marissa's timid tongue darted out to lick Donovan's lips and the fire that had smoldered all day erupted, causing Donovan to crush her breasts against his chest and start his tongue on a journey to learn the secrets of her moist, cavernous mouth. They kissed hungrily, searching, and then with a reverence-filled lightness. When they stopped, Marissa looked at Donovan, her eyes glistening with threatening tears. "This feels scary," she whispered in a raw, honest moment. "It's almost taking my breath away."

"That's how love feels, baby," Donovan said, taking a loose tendril of her hair and placing it behind her ear. "Like you can hardly breathe." She helped him remove his shirt and then his pants. And then each of them tossed aside their underwear before stepping into a shower large enough to hose down a small army.

Donovan made sure the water was just right before he pulled Marissa into the rain shower, where the talking stopped and the kissing resumed. He reached for the liquid soap and loofah sponge and proceeded to sculpt Marissa's body as if it were a Michelangelo masterpiece. He washed every inch of her, his lips and tongue following the sponge, until she was shivering first from desire and then from the intensity of her release. Again she marveled at what she'd been missing, all of those years she'd gone wanting and unfulfilled without even knowing what was missing from her life. No wonder he'd looked at her strangely when she talked of taking or leaving sexual pleasure. Because at this moment, Marissa couldn't imagine life without loving ever again.

She finally came back down to earth, still clinging to Donovan's body. She loved the feel of him, how he was in shape and toned, but how he wasn't so defined that his body resembled a cartoon character. She loved how there was meat on his bones, and how his thighs were thick and strong and powerful. After a second shower, the couple skinny-dipped in Donovan's infinity pool. They made love under the stars and fell asleep in a hammock made for two. For Marissa it was paradise, and there was nowhere in the world she'd rather be.

After a leisurely Saturday that mostly alternated between love-making, movie watching and long conversations, a ravenous Marissa and Donovan awoke on Sunday and ambled into the kitchen for energy-replenishing food. While he scoured the fridge, she sat at the massive island in his kitchen, downing strong coffee to combat very little shut-eye and marveling at how quickly her life had changed. Anyone who'd told her two weeks ago that today she would have been in a half-naked man's kitchen watching him fix eggs, well, she would have wondered what they were smoking.

She placed her elbow on the table and her chin in her palm as she watched him, a warm and fuzzy feeling going from her head to her toes. In an instant, she was transported back to childhood and the rare morning when her father would fix breakfast, the only meal he could prepare. She looked at the clock. It was just before ten. As hard as it was to pull herself away, she really wanted to go to church and felt that if she ate quickly, then left within the hour, she could get there in time for the sermon to begin.

The companionable silence continued as she watched Donovan add the vegetables he'd julienned into the egg mixture, along with a generous helping of cheese. That done, he placed the bread he'd buttered into the oven, then flipped a portion of the egg over to create an enviable omelet. A few minutes later, he winked at her. "Breakfast is served."

They decided to keep it casual and eat at the island. Conversation was sparse in the beginning, as each worked to replenish the calories they'd burned off during last night's aerobics. At one point, Marissa looked up to see Donovan watching her, something she'd observed several times in their two full days together.

"Why do you do that?"

"Do what?"

"Watch me like that."

"Does it bother you?"

"Sometimes it makes me feel like I've got a third eye growing in my forehead or something."

"Ha! I don't mean to make you uncomfortable. I just find you intriguing, that's all."

"How so?" she asked around a forkful of omelet.

"Like the fact that before we were together, you'd never had an orgasm."

"I never should have said anything."

"No, baby. I'm glad you told me." He paused and reached for her hand, rubbed her palm with his strong thumb. "It's almost like you were a virgin and I was your first." He reached over and wiped a crumb from the side of Marissa's mouth, then outlined it with her finger, before delivering a light peck.

"Can I ask you something?"

"Yes but—"

"I know," she said, before making her voice gruff in a poor replica of Donovan's tone, "Doesn't mean a Drake man is going to answer it."

"Ask me anything, baby."

"What happened with the woman you said you almost married, the one who hurt you?" Marissa noted Donovan's immediate change of mood, how those eyes so intense and expressive became hooded and cold. "It's okay, you don't have to tell me."

"No, I want to. I don't want there to be any secrets between us." He said that, but continued eating, so much so that Marissa thought that he'd decided against it after all. But finally he put down his fork and crossed his arms as he leaned back in his bar stool. "She became pregnant with my child and terminated the pregnancy without my consent."

Marissa's reaction was a startled gasp. "No!" she breathed. Having watched the pride on Donovan's face whenever he talked about the Drakes, from their colorful past to their bright-looking future, she could only imagine how this had made him feel. "How did you find out?"

"We'd dated for five years, had known each other for longer than that. I knew Erica, her moods, her personality, her body. I'd noticed she was gaining weight, not a lot, not even enough for the average person to tell, but for whatever reason I noticed it. But when I commented about it, she brushed me off. I mentioned it to my mother and she's the first one who brought up the fact that she might be pregnant. Erica assured me that she was not. But about two, three weeks later, she went out of town—" Donovan used air quotes "—and when she came back, she just wasn't the same. She'd been gone about a week and the next time I saw her, that little extra weight I'd noticed was gone. I kept bugging her about it until she lost her temper and told me."

"I'm sorry, Donovan."

"Yeah, me, too. For me, it was the ultimate betrayal. Anybody who could do that to my seed could not be my wife."

They were silent then, for a long time. When Marissa spoke, her statement was telling. "I love children," she said.

A short time later, as Marissa drove to Blessed Assurance, she thought about Donovan and the baby he'd lost. She thought about the man that she'd gained, the one she no longer wished to run from. At the same time, she refused to consider a future with a threat constantly dangled over her head. If Steven McCain was at church today, she'd face her accuser. It was time to call his bluff, to put her past behind her once and for all.

Because of a special baptism, Marissa caught the entire church service. The music was great, the message uplifting and her spirit of hope was fortified. By the time they'd reached the benediction, she was more than ready for Steven. So much so, that when she saw Antonio, she walked right up.

"Hey, Antonio."

"Hey, Marissa!"

"Where's Steven?"

"I have no idea and could care even less," Antonio said, with a frown. "After what happened with y'all a week ago, we had a falling out. I told him his actions were inappropriate. He told me to go to hell."

"I'm sorry, Antonio."

"It is what it is."

"I don't know what's happened to Steven. He isn't the same guy I used to know. I'm going to keep praying for him though. With God, all things are possible."

"Well, that's who's going to have to help him. 'Cause I'm done."

Little did Marissa know that shortly, she'd be done, too.

Chapter 27

It had only been two weeks since she'd last been there, but Monday morning found Marissa feeling out of sorts as she pulled into the Boss Construction parking lot, the place of her employ for the last several years. How was it that she could miss a place where she'd only spent two weeks while the place that had often served as her home away from home now seemed foreign? She looked over and found some comfort in seeing a familiar sight: a black Jeep Cherokee back in its spot. The honeymoon was over. Boss was back at work.

After greeting several of her coworkers she continued on to her work area, which was just beyond Jackson's door. "Good morning," she said to him, bypassing her desk area and walking straight through his opened door. "How does it feel to sit in that chair as a married man?"

"Same way it felt the day before I walked down the aisle," Jackson replied, scrolling through what was undoubtedly hundreds of emails, looking for emergencies while leaving spam and other run-of-the-mill correspondence for Marissa to sort out later. "What about you?" he said at last, taking his eyes from the computer screen and leaning back in his chair. "Looks like life at the resort agreed with you?"

Marissa felt herself grow warm and hoped she wasn't blushing. Was the satiated and satisfied way she felt written all over her face? "I don't have to tell you how amazing that place is," she replied, after gathering a batch of mail from his desk and sitting down just to buy time. "Seeing as how you built it and all."

Jackson nodded. "So how was it working with Donovan?"

His question was asked casually but, knowing the Drakes the way Donovan had explained them, she thought that her love life might have been a topic of conversation between him and Diamond as soon as they landed at LAX and listened to voice mails. "It was fine," was her accurate answer, however brief.

"Then I guess I should ask…how was playing with him?" Jackson could no longer keep the straight face and broke out into a grin.

Marissa looked behind her and then got up and closed the door. "Okay, Boss, out with it. Just what did Donovan tell Diamond and how much do you already know?"

"Donovan didn't have to tell us anything. Hearing that you attended the family gathering was a pretty big 4-1-1. Looking into your dreamy eyes is another FYI."

"Is it that obvious?"

"It is for someone like me, who's known you for as long as I have." Jackson turned serious. "Are you sure this is a good idea, Marissa? I know it's none of my business, but considering the dynamics I am already involved. For the record, I think Donovan is a good man. And I obviously vouch for the Drakes as a great family, since I became a recent card-carrying member. But considering what you've been through—"

"Donovan isn't like the others," Marissa interrupted.

Jackson nodded. "Okay. I get it. I know when to butt out."

"I'm sorry, Boss. It's just that…whatever this is with me and Donovan, it's different. Not like your average relationship, you know?"

Jackson held up his ring finger. "Trust me, I know." They laughed and the uncomfortable moment passed. "How was it living at the resort for two weeks?"

"Like a dream."

"I don't have to worry about you leaving me, do I? Don't have to think about jacking Donovan up for stealing my assistant?"

Marissa laughed. The phone rang, signaling an end to their banter and the beginning of her workday. She answered the phone on his desk. "Good morning, Jackson Wright's office." She waited. "Oh, hello, Mr. Laurent. Yes, he's right here. One moment, please." She placed the call on hold.

Jackson took the receiver but paused before taking the call off hold. "You didn't answer my question. Do I need to start looking for another assistant?"

"Naw, Boss. For now, you're pretty much stuck with me."

* * *

Across town, a similar conversation was being conducted. "Boy, I can't leave you alone for a minute!" Diamond had breezed past Donovan's assistant, walked in his office and shut the door.

"Good morning to you, too, sis. And, yes, please do join me in my office."

"Thank you, I think I will," Diamond replied, already sitting down. "So go ahead. Give me all of the details."

"All of the details to what?" Donovan continued looking through the report on his desk and sipping his coffee without a care.

"To the message Mom left on my phone, about you and Marissa being an item. What's the backstory? Because that was a fast move, bro, even for a Drake man!"

"If I remember correctly, somebody named Wright moved pretty fast."

"We're not talking about me. It's all about you right now. So," she prompted when he remained silent. "What happened?"

"Yes," Dexter asked, entering the office just as she asked the question. "What went down in Drake Wines Resort and Spa town?"

Donovan sighed and leaned back in his chair. "Isn't it Monday morning, and don't you two have things to do? Dexter, your production load is about to increase about fiftyfold. I can't imagine that you have a speck of free time. Diamond, you've been out of the office for two weeks. It's a wonder you moved past the work piled in your office to get out the door."

"You're right, brother. I am back, and I am swamped. Which is why you should talk fast. Kat already told me as much as she knows, I just need you to fill in a few blanks."

Donovan drawled, "Oh, Lord. The Kat is out the bag."

Dexter's phone rang. "Yes," he said, speaking to his assistant. "Okay, that's fine. Get them settled into one of the private dining rooms. I'll be over shortly. You're saved by the bell, brother." Dexter rose. "But don't think you're off the hook."

"What about you? We're still wondering about the woman Mom said was on your arm over the weekend."

"Onyx? Ah, that's a hot sister right there!"

Diamond stood. "That's my cue. I surely don't have time right now for a rundown of your conquests of the past two weeks. But what say you guys come over to our house for dinner tonight? I'm feeling the need for a sibling powwow."

"That sounds like a plan," Donovan said, reaching for his organizer.

"Count me in," Dexter said, heading for the door.

Diamond fell into step beside him, placed her arm around his waist. "We'll also talk later about the international," she threw over her shoulder. "I scanned the report. I guess you did as well as you could without me."

Donovan smirked as he raised his eyes to meet Diamond's dancing ones. "Welcome back, sis," he said sarcastically. "We really missed you."

Within hours at Boss Construction, Marissa was back into the swing of things. She'd handled all of Jackson's time-sensitive messages and, after grabbing a water and juice from the break room, settled into her chair for the next massive project: sifting through two weeks' worth of emails.

Deciding to break this job into chunks, she first decided to do a quick scan and delete as many scam mails that had missed her junk folder. Almost three hundred were deleted with that first sweep. Next, she checked the ones she knew were valid and placed them in a separate folder. She'd get to their particulars once she was done. That left about a hundred messages that she needed to open and read, to make sure she didn't delete something the company needed. She'd gone through about half of those when, while yawning, she clicked on a message titled "Information Requested." And almost fell out of her chair.

Five pictures.

Five poses.

Marissa naked, flaunting. And in one…

She quickly closed the window and reached for her purse. "Boss, I'm going to lunch," she said once she'd punched the intercom button. Seconds later, she was out the door. She didn't know what she was going to do, but she had to do something. Because if those pictures saw the light of day…life as she knew it was a wrap.

"Marissa?" Donovan had looked once, then again, when he saw her walk through his office door. With it being Boss's first day back, he wasn't sure he'd see her today, or tonight for that matter. They'd been burning the candle at both ends. He'd already made peace with the fact that she needed sleep and his bed tonight might feel empty. But here she was. And something was wrong.

He got up and closed the door, then reached for her hand and led them over to the sitting area of his office.

Leaning over, he hit the speaker button and spoke to the temp now covering for Sharon. "Hold my calls." That done he leaned against the couch, slowly rubbing Marissa's hand. "Talk to me."

Gently pulling her hand away, Marissa began speaking, staring straight ahead. "Remember when you asked me about being a preacher's kid and if there'd ever been a time when I rebelled?"

"Yes."

"I said that while in college, I'd done something I wished I hadn't." Tears threatened. Marissa swallowed them back, clenching her teeth to help staunch the flow. Crying would not help this situation. She doubted that anything would. "I posed once, nude, for an art class."

Five seconds passed. Ten. Twenty.

"That's it?" Relief was palpable in his voice. "Baby, the human body is nothing to be ashamed of."

"That's not the point!" *Deep breaths, Marissa. In. Out. Donovan is not the problem here.* "What I mean is, growing up with the beliefs that were taught in my home, exposing one's body was a very big deal. But at the time, I was toying with the idea of being a model. I mean, at one time or another doesn't every girl want to do that?" A single tear escaped Marissa's control, slid down her face and plopped onto her blouse. "I told Steven about my dream and a couple weeks later, he told me about the class. It took a while, but he convinced me to at least think about it, said it would be a great way to get experience, help me lose my inhibitions and shyness at being looked at, standing in front of a crowd. Yes, I'd sang and spoken in front of the church. But I'd grown up with those people, had known them all my life!

"I went to the class and spoke with the teacher. She

assured me that there would only be drawings, that no cameras or video equipment were ever allowed. But Steven had set up a camera that could shoot into the dressing room where I changed." She turned to face Donovan. Another tear fell. "He caught me…doing things I shouldn't. Adopting naughty poses and…touching myself." Donovan said nothing, but again he reached for her hand. This time, she didn't pull away. "He has pictures, Donovan. And he's threatening to post them on the internet if I don't…"

"Don't what?" Donovan's voice was calm, deadly calm.

Her answer was barely above a whisper. "Sleep with him."

"That's not going to happen."

"But how do I stop him? The pictures are already digital, he sent them to my work email! He's never gotten over the fact that I wouldn't date him and that I got a promotion he felt should have been his. He'll do it, Donovan, I know he will! He said he'd send them to members of my dad's congregation. His television ministry, my mother…oh, God!"

Donovan took her into his arms, wanting to take away her pain and then take Steven's life. "I'm here, baby. I've got you. I know this situation looks unbearable, but we'll get through it together."

Donovan's words were like a dagger in Marissa's heart. She sat straight up. "Oh, no."

"What?"

"He can't know that we're together. That was another part of the threat, that if he ever saw me with anyone else he'd expose me, ruin me, for not being with him." Marissa's eyes filled with despair along with the tears.

This time, she didn't even try and stop their flow. "I'm so sorry, Donovan." Her voice was raspy, aching with emotion. "I can't do this to you, to your family."

Donovan took Marissa firmly by the shoulders. "Baby, stop it. Listen to me. Look at me. My sweet, sweet Marissa. Baby, look at me." She did. "The Drakes have been in plenty of battles. We don't lose many, and we never run from fights. I'm not going to leave you. My family will not leave you. We're going to get this handled. And I promise you—" he took her chin in his hand, forced the eye contact "—I promise you that this Steven dude will rue the day he crossed you. He's getting ready to find out that when he messes with you, he's messing with me. For him, that's not a good look."

"But your family, Donovan? I'm so embarrassed."

"Nothing to be ashamed of, sweetness. They love you now. They'll love you later."

After another thirty minutes, he sent a slightly less frazzled Marissa to La Jolla with a key to his home. "Don't worry about Boss," he'd told her. He too was family and would understand the need to circle the wagons. And in very short order, Donovan did just that. He pulled Dexter and his father into his office and before they could take a seat informed them, "We've got a situation."

Chapter 28

The next day, and at Donovan's suggestion, Marissa found herself in Naperville, Illinois, sitting in her parents' grandiose living room. Last night had been a whirlwind as she, Donovan, Diamond and Jackson strategized on how to handle Steven, how to ensure that the pictures would be destroyed. Jackson contacted a private eye, Frank Stanton, "an old codger who would wade through a minefield to get a lead." Knowing that a good offense was a great defense they hoped to scour Steven's closet for a skeleton or two. Diamond had looked at the pictures in order to give an objective opinion from a woman's point of view. "There's plenty worse that's out there," she offered, after seeing Marissa's bare backside, breasts and more. And then, "Girl, I'm not gay but your body's tight! No wonder my brother's all twisted." This comment delivered one of the few laughs of the night.

And this morning, the Drakes' car service had picked her up and taken her to the airport, and she was now seated in first-class for an early morning flight to Chicago. All she'd told her mother was that she was on her way to share something and it involved Steven. Thankfully, her father wasn't out of town. She hadn't wanted to have to share this story twice. But she shared it. And never had she endured a silence as long as the one happening now, after just baring her soul and her shame to her perfect mother and mega-minister dad. She sat back and waited, spent and empty. And while she felt horrible for having had to reveal a secret she'd hoped would go to the grave, she also felt strangely relieved, almost liberated, like removing a huge weight after carrying it around for a while. For almost ten years to be exact.

Finally her father, Reverend Sam Hayes, broke the silence. "I'm sorry this has happened, Marissa. Sorry that you're hurting, and that something that was done in relative darkness has come to light. But what was done in the past cannot be undone now. We'll just have to deal with what happens, whatever it is, and keep moving. We'll get through this, daughter. But I want you to do something for me. I want you to remember that nobody's perfect, and we were all young once. Your mother and I have done things that we'd take back if we could. Everyone has." Marissa's eyes registered surprise. Her father continued, "Yes, I know you and your brother think we're perfect. That's our fault, keeping you sheltered the way we did, not wanting you to know when we were going through things. But you're an adult, where we now might share things that we didn't before. Am I fine with what's happened? Of course not. Do I wish you'd made a different choice? Certainly. But you've asked for

forgiveness and thus have nothing to be ashamed of."
He put a firm hand on her shoulder. "Wipe your tears
and hold your head up, Marissa. This too shall pass."

"He's right, baby," Yolanda said, coming to sit beside
her daughter. "Before we're a ministry, we're a family. And whatever that scoundrel Steven does, we'll get
through this together."

Marissa was stunned speechless. She'd imagined
many scenarios of what would happen if her parents
ever found out she'd posed nude and now, even worse,
that Steven was threatening to post pictures he'd se-
cretly shot of her online. None of the images had looked
like this, her parents calm and understanding, offering
compassion instead of judgment. She'd continued talking with them then, in the most open and heartfelt conversation with her parents she'd ever had. And when
she left Chicago, it was with the strength to face Steven
McCain…and whatever else.

Meanwhile, back at the vineyard, Donovan conferred
with his father. Donald had taken an immediate liking
to Marissa, saying her quiet, observant demeanor reminded him a bit of Genevieve.

"Did you see them?" Donald asked, having told Donovan that that was the first thing he needed to do. Know
firsthand exactly what they were up against. Donovan
nodded.

"What do you think?"

"They were taken years ago, when she was just nine-
teen. Pretty tame by today's standards. But her father's
high profile in ministry makes the situation all the more
tenuous. She's more afraid of embarrassing him and
causing a scandal than fearing for her own reputation."

"What do you know about this guy?"

"Nothing more than what Marissa has told me. He grew up in Long Beach. They met in college. He wanted to date her, she didn't, but they became friends. Later he helped get her hired at the company where he still works." Donovan finished by relaying the date drug incident. "It's fools like him that give men a bad name."

"Son, the person you just described is not a real man. He's a coward, one who needs to be taught a lesson." After a brief pause, he continued, "We need to learn everything we can about this punk. You have to know your opponent to defeat your opponent."

Donovan smiled. "Already got Boss's guy working on it. Frank Stanton, the detective who helped him last year."

"Good." Donald was silent a moment, thoughtfully puffing his cigar. "You say you know where he works?"

"Yes."

"Be good to know if we can work from that angle. Cut off the money, and you can cut off the man."

As he left his father's study and walked back to the office, the wheels in Donovan's strategic mind were whirling. His father had a point. Donovan had a plan. It had taken a lifetime to find her and nobody was going to come between him and this chance at real love. Nobody.

Exactly one week later, Steven McCain arrived home to find company that he had not invited. An official-looking character in a suit and a not-so-official-looking character in sweats engaged him in conversation, saying they had an offer that he shouldn't refuse. A large firearm pointed in the general vicinity of vital body parts was a strong incentive for Steven to play along.

"You know the pictures we're looking for," Mr. Official explained. "We've already swept the electronics here and deleted the images. Should there be others, it would be in your best interest to let us know where they are so that we can make sure they are destroyed." Mr. Not-So-Official-Looking raised the "incentive" from Steven's chest to his face.

"I won't do nothing with them," Steven stuttered.

"That's not quite the response I was looking for." Mr. Not-So took a step. "Are there any other devices containing photos of Marissa Hayes?"

"My, uh, my cell phone."

"Where is it?"

"Look, I just got it. Cost me six hundred bucks!"

"Oh, yeah?" Mr. Official's tone was as casual as if he were discussing a sport. "How much is your life worth?"

Steven gave him the phone.

The men finished one last piece of business and then left with these parting words: should any pictures of questionable content involving Marissa Hayes ever surface, whether taken by him or someone else, he would be held accountable. The punishments mentioned varied from jail time to heavy fines, to the one that Mr. Not-So held against his head for five minutes before leaving. Incentive, he'd called it.

Indeed.

An hour after Steven's uninvited visitors left his apartment, Frank Stanton, Jackson and Dexter knocked on Donovan's door. Frank held a manila envelope, which he presented as soon as he stepped inside.

"He signed it?"

Frank nodded. "Of course."

"How'd you do it?"

"I didn't. But I have friends. They have a way with… words, if you will."

"Speaking of words, I think Steven and I still need to have a conversation."

"That's why I called Frank, bro, and Dexter," Jackson said. "So we could come here with him when the job was done. I knew you wouldn't be satisfied with having him handle this for you. That you'd want to have a go at him yourself."

"The guy's such a jerk I may still get my chance."

Dexter placed a hand on his brother's shoulder. "No doubt, Don. But now's not the time. He's not worth the millions we stand to lose if negative publicity hits Drake Wines right now. And he's not worth your worrying Marissa."

Donovan fixed Dexter with a look. "That's the best thing you could say to make me back off of him."

Dexter winked at Jackson and nodded at Frank. "I know, big brother. I know."

Marissa sat across from Donovan, the flicker of the candle highlighting the glow on his face. She was drinking in the man who, after she'd taken a stand and unlocked the chain of guilt and fear that Steven had wrapped around her, had ridden in like a knight in shining armor and made her boogeyman disappear. Donovan wouldn't tell her exactly what he and his family did to make Steven sign legal documents preventing further harassment, but she'd forever thank him for it.

As for Donovan, he marveled at the woman across from him, the one who in just two short weeks had taken him from a single man content to bury himself in work and in a woman when the mood struck him, to one beginning to think in terms of *we* and not *I*. Words were not needed in the moment. They were content to simply sit there, smiling, taking each other in.

The sommelier came to the table, breaking the mood. "Monsieur, may I?" He held up the bottle of pricey champagne and, after popping the cork, poured a bit into Donovan's flute.

Donovan sampled it and nodded. "Perfect."

After filling the two flutes, the sommelier placed the remainder of the bubbly back into the ice bucket and left the table as quietly as he'd come.

"A toast?" Donovan suggested, picking up his glass. Marissa followed suit, her face alight with happiness.

"To new beginnings?" she offered.

Donovan nodded. "To you and me."

Marissa's smile broadened. "I like the sound of that." They drank a couple sips in silence before she continued, "I can't believe how good it feels to take control of your life, to feel that you're actually driving your own destiny. I didn't even realize that for the past several years, I've just been drifting through, content to let others take the reins, to go along to get along. But no more. From now on, I'm my own woman."

"Just as long as that includes being my woman, too."

As they enjoyed courses of oysters on the half shell and organic kale, abalone mushroom and double-cut chops, the conversation slowly drifted away from nude pics and bad guys to vacations and wine.

"You've never been out of the country?"

"No, Donovan, I never have. And don't look so incredulous. Eighty percent of Americans don't travel farther than two states over from where they were born."

"That's baloney."

"I read it."

"Can't believe it."

Marissa shrugged. "When are we going to get a chance to taste that bubbly that Dexter's been working on for years? It's like he's a mad scientist, perfecting his potion."

"Have you seen him in action? That's exactly what he's like."

"Speaking of action…"

"I know, baby. Me, too." In the swirl of the whirlwind—Jackson winning the Louisiana bid; Sharon returning to her home in Temecula and back to the office, at her insistence, two hours a day for the next two weeks; Marissa returning to Boss Construction; and the Drake clan dealing with what's his name—there had been a noticeable void in the romance department. One that Donovan planned to fill just a short while from now.

Less than an hour after arriving at Donovan's home he and Marissa were naked and playing pool. Her dare. "I like how you're working that stick, sweetness," he said after she'd sunk a ball in a way that would have made a pool shark proud. He especially liked how she'd looked leaning over to sink it, breasts swaying like melons, booty high in the air.

Donovan didn't mention this to her, but one look at his other stick and she got the message all the same. She sauntered over, placed a brazen hand on his baby maker. "How would you like for me to work…this stick?"

"Um, baby, I like how you think."

"Hmm," she sank down until she was face-to-face with her focus. "Would you like me to do this?" She flicked her tongue against his personal portobello.

"Um, yeah."

"What about this?" She stiffened her tongue and licked him slowly from base to tip.

"Damn, girl, you've got me all excited."

"What about…" Figuring actions spoke louder, she quieted, taking as much of him in as she could. His groans, thrusts and the way he massaged her head let her know that though she was pretty much a novice, she was doing a good job.

So much so that Donovan stopped the action, pulled out of her mouth. "Baby…it feels so good that…"

Marissa chuckled. "Okay. How's about if we find another use for this pool table?"

Without another word, Donovan lifted Marissa up onto the table, and proceeded to once again work his stick.

Chapter 29

It was a boisterous gathering at the Drake family's dining room table, almost twenty people vying for a break in the conversation, when they could pipe in with their two cents. Having grown up in a relatively small household of four, Marissa still marveled at how all of the conversation strands could be kept straight, how one sibling would finish the other's sentence and how one mate could finish another's story.

It had been four months since that fateful Fourth of July eve, four glorious months since she and Donovan had made the transition from professional associates to lovers. Whether four months or four lifetimes, she couldn't tell. All she knew is that it seemed as though he'd been a part of her life forever and that she couldn't remember life before he was in it. She couldn't be happier, especially looking over to see her mother, brother and sister-in-law also at the table. Her father had wanted to come but because of the annual Thanksgiving service held at his church, had to decline the invitation. The compromise was that Donovan had agreed to spend Christmas with Marissa's family, which Marissa was positive would be a much quieter affair, filled with good cheer but without the loud laughter that even now echoed around the room thanks to Papa Dee and his colorful tales.

"What about that time you beat up a man for insulting your girlfriend, Papa Dee?"

"And found out he was one of Capone's boys?" Papa Dee dismissed its significance with a wave of his hand. "Ah, that wasn't nothing. You should have been there when I slapped the taste out of Bugsy Siegel's mouth!"

Marissa's eyes widened in wonder. "Really, Papa Dee? You rolled with gangsters?"

"Girl, my great-grandson hasn't told you? These young whippersnappers got it all twisted. I'm a *true* OG!"

Laughter abounded and the stories flowed. Half of them real, others heavily doctored, but all shared to enhance the family's good time. They stayed around the table for a good two hours, but finally the crowd began dissipating. Some of the men headed to the golf course, while others joined Donald for a Cuban cigar. Marissa joined in with the ladies who were clearing the table, feeling at home with Donovan's warm relations.

She picked up a platter of leftover vegetables and another of rolls and walked them into the kitchen. "How should I store these, Mrs. Drake?"

"Don't worry about it, sweetheart. The housekeeper will take care of all that. Why don't you join us in the sitting room for a cup of tea. What kind would you like?"

"Whatever you're having is fine."

Several minutes later, Genevieve entered the sitting room wheeling a cart bearing tea and condiments. The ladies shared small talk as they each fixed their cups. For Genevieve, it was two dollops of honey and a splash of cream in a simple green tea. She stirred the mixture, eyeing Marissa with a smile on her face. "I knew it," she finally said, nodding.

"Excuse me?"

"The first time I saw you, no, not the first time. Because I met you at the grand opening. But the night of the engagement party, when I saw you I knew. I told Donald that something was brewing between you and Donovan. I saw the way he looked at you when he didn't know I was watching. I know my son, know how he is when he gets his mind set on something. And the way I saw him looking at you that night, I could tell he had his mind set."

"I didn't even know he was watching."

"That was the best part. I've watched the women over the years with my sons. Most of them couldn't be more obvious about being interested if they took out a commercial on national TV. This new type of aggressiveness being the modern way to get a man's attention. And it may be. But not with a Drake man. Those brothers are old-school, they like to do the hunting." She winked at Marissa. "Donovan has a real pep in his step these days. You've made him very happy."

"Thank you, Mrs. Drake. I appreciate that. But can I tell you something? Your son has made me pretty happy, too."

And he wasn't finished yet. Mr. Drake had plans.

* * *

"Donovan," Marissa whispered. "Where are we going?" It was just past midnight and for the first time Marissa was staying at the Drake estate. Genevieve had placed her in Diamond's old room, which now served as a beautifully appointed guest room. Though Donovan had moved out years ago, his mother still maintained his old room in another wing of the house. He'd waited there until relatively sure his parents were sleeping before leaving his room and creeping over to the east wing to wake up his princess. "Donovan, where are we going?" Marissa asked again.

Donovan placed a finger to his lips to signal quiet. Marissa put a hand over her mouth to stifle a giggle. She hadn't felt this way, sneaky and naughty, since she was eight years old and she and her brother had tried to sneak into their parents' closet and discover their Christmas toys. The house was mostly dark and quiet, shards of light were given off by the dimly lit sconces and, once they'd turned the corner, by the full moon shining through the great-room window.

They reached the foyer. Donovan opened the closet door and pulled out jackets for him and Marissa.

"We're going outside?"

Donovan chuckled as he looked at Marissa's feet and then reached inside for a pair of closed-in shoes. "You ask too many questions, woman!"

"It's after midnight, and it's cold outside. I should be asking questions!"

He knelt down, placing her feet into her shoes while ducking the light punches she delivered to his shoulder. Once standing, he grabbed her butt and pulled her to him, lightly kissed her on the mouth and then gave a final smack to her now jacket-covered backside. "Let's go."

They stepped outside, and a burst of cold made Marissa pull the large jacket tighter. Donovan reached over for her, engulfing her small hand with his much larger one, entwining their fingers as he kissed her on the temple. She nestled into his warmth. With both the jacket and his body shielding her from the brunt of the wind, she looked out on the magical scene before her and actually began to appreciate their midnight rendezvous.

From the moment the lights were turned on Thanksgiving night, Drake Wines Resort and Spa had been transformed into a winter wonderland. Thousands of miniature white lights sparkled amid the pine boughs; not one tree was left untouched. A huge Christmas tree had been erected on the large open area between the hotel and the wine store, the tree trunks had been wrapped in bright red satin that was then secured by giant bows. Not to be outdone, the stars twinkled their approval and the sky was like a blanket of blue velvet. Marissa couldn't remember a time when she'd been happier in her life.

They reached the fork in the road from the Drake estate. One path led toward the businesses, including the hotel, another toward the Papa Dee Suite on the hill. And yet another led back to a private area owned by the family. That was the direction that Donovan headed. They hadn't gone far when Marissa heard something that stopped her in her tracks: a horse's whinny.

"Are we going riding?" she squealed, clapping her hands together like a little girl. Of all the things in his world that Donovan had introduced her to, riding horses was probably her favorite. He taught her himself how to ride, a patient and thorough teacher. Normally she rode Miss America, the horse that Diego had recommended on her very first ride. But that didn't sound like her.

"Which horse am I riding?" she asked. "Sauvignon?"

"You'll see."

They turned the corner and came upon a wooden enclosure. Here, away from the brighter lights of the Christmas decorations, it was darker. Donovan produced a flashlight from his pocket and illuminated the path in front of them. Now Marissa could clearly see there were two horses—Zephyr, who she'd know anywhere, and another one. With a bright red bow wrapped around it. She stopped, her mouth open in total surprise.

"Is this for me?" she whispered, loosening Donovan's hand and walking toward the horse.

"It was planned as a Christmas present, but my contact was able to get her delivered earlier. I didn't want to wait a month for you two to meet. Baby, here." Donovan reached over and gave her a bag of apple slices. "Go make your acquaintance."

Marissa smiled her thanks. Even in the subdued lighting she could see how beautiful the horse was; its rich, shiny coat was a tawny brown and it had a thick black mane to match the curious eyes now staring at her as if to say, *Do I belong to you?* Marissa's steps were calm as was her breathing, done as Donovan had explained to her, so that the horse would recognize her calmness and feel the same. Stopping when she was just a foot or so away from it, she reached over and began to slowly stroke the horse's side, talking softly as she did so. "Hello there, you beautiful girl. What a beautiful horse you are. Would you like an apple?" She held up the apple under the horse's nose. It sniffed the slice, its eyes never leaving Marissa's face, and slowly began to nibble. "There you go." Tears filled her eyes as she petted the animal. It was such a thoughtful gift. She turned to Donovan. "Thank you."

"She isn't totally yours until you ride her," he said softly. Knowing how jealous Zephyr could be, he'd gone over and fed the stallion a few carrots before coming over to stand next to Marissa.

"You want to ride now? Tonight?"

"Yes. And if it weren't so cold, I'd want you to ride naked."

"Ha! This isn't Coventry and I am not Lady Godiva."

"No, but you are a pretty sweet piece of chocolate." He reached out and stroked her horse's mane. "What are you going to name her?"

She looked at the horse and cocked her head in thought. "I don't know. I'm going to have to think about that." Walking over to him, she placed her arms around Donovan's neck. "What did I do to deserve you?" she asked.

"Be born," he replied simply before lowering his head to connect his lips with hers. Their tongues swirled in practiced rhythm. Feeling himself beginning to harden, Donovan broke the kiss. "Come on, there's something I want to show you."

After admiring the amazing soft and supple saddle that Donovan had given her along with the horse as her early Christmas presents, she readied the horse that was not yet named. They mounted the animals and set off in a comfortable pace toward Papa Dee's Suite. "Isn't someone there?" she asked.

"No," Donovan said. "I booked it months ago, the day we drank the bottle of wine up on the mountain."

Marissa's brow rose as she glanced over at Donovan. "Sure of yourself much?"

Donovan shrugged. "No." But he was smiling, "cheesing," as his father would say.

They arrived at Papa Dee's Suite, the house that had been built by Donovan's great-great-grandfather, Nicodemus in the nineteenth century. Like the rest of the properties, it had been totally renovated, but Jackson and his crew had been careful to not change the integrity of what their ancestor had designed. They dismounted and, after throwing their reins over the original post, he walked the length of the long front porch and pulled a key from his pocket. "Are you ready?"

Marissa hesitated. Why, she didn't know. She'd wanted to see Papa Dee's Suite but it had always been occupied on her earlier visits. This was no surprise, considering the popularity of the resort as a wedding destination. She'd read the brochure, which included the home's humble beginnings, had tried to imagine Donovan's ancestor, Nicodemus laying plank upon plank and brick upon brick by the sweat of his brow with Mamie, his wife, cooking hearty stews in a cast iron pot hanging over the fireplace. She'd imagined also being lifted over the door's threshold on her wedding night, had thought that that was when she'd lay eyes on the interior beyond her. Somehow, it felt awkward to go in now.

"I thought this suite was for newlyweds," she finally said.

"Mostly," Donovan replied. "But I have to let you in on a tradition, newly started by Jackson and my sister. You see, the average guest takes advantage of this home's wonderful amenities after they get married. But in the Drake family's unique fashion, we've chosen to sample its luxuries before we walk down the aisle."

"Who are you planning to walk down the aisle with?" Marissa said, her face close to Donovan's, her demeanor uncharacteristically sassy. "Since I'm not wearing a ring?"

"You've been hanging too much around Diamond," Donovan murmured, not unpleased. He unlocked the door. "It's bringing out your feisty side. But make no mistake, I'm still running things." With that he swooped her up, causing a whoosh of air to escape from her lips. She wrapped her hands tightly around Donovan's neck as he walked them over the threshold into a quaint, square living room that had been obviously renovated yet clearly maintained its original design. Gleaming hardwood floors, a pressed brick fireplace and silk-covered walls with a floral design immediately transported the guest back in time. A Victorian-style couch with curved wooden legs and deep burgundy velvet sat beneath the paned front window, a quilted throw at the ready to block out the chill. Topping off this seamless step back in time was the roaring fireplace with small logs crackling as they burned and fell to the charred remains below.

"It's officially over, but Happy Thanksgiving, Marissa." Donovan smiled.

"But when…how?" She turned around, taking in the room, including a bottle of champagne cooling in a silver bucket. "That's why you left," she continued, thinking back to earlier in the evening when, as the family sipped mugs of hot chocolate in the great room, Donovan had excused himself. He'd been gone for about half an hour. *Looks like somebody had been busy.*

"This is the most amazing thing that anybody has ever done for me," she said, tears in her eyes. "And I'm very thankful. I love you, Donovan." *Oops? Did the three little words just come out of my mouth? Maybe I said it in my mind and thought I said it out loud.* But the big smile on Donovan's face told another story.

"I'll toast to that!" he said. He walked over to the table holding the champagne bucket. "You're in for a treat," he told her. "This is from the first batch of the new champagne that Dexter and Papa Dee produced. It's an exclusive bottle, very expensive. It won't even be sold in regular stores."

"Oh! The Diamond!" Marissa laughed, feeling giddy that she would be one of the first to taste the bubbly that was her boyfriend's sister's namesake.

He uncorked the bottle and after pouring them each a flute he walked over and handed one to Marissa. "I had no idea that when this year started it would end this way, with a special woman by my side, and by me asking the most important question of my life." He set down the glass.

As he began to kneel, Marissa began to tremble. *No! Is he going to...yes! He is!* She, too, set down her glass, continuing to look at Donovan with love in her eyes.

"Marissa Drake, I know we haven't dated a long time. But Papa Dee says when it's right, it don't take long. And I believe this is right. Will you marry me?"

"Yes!" she said before the last word had barely left his mouth. "Yes, yes, yes!" He stood then, capturing Marissa's mouth in a bruising kiss, lapping up her love, drinking her in as though he could never get enough. When the kiss ended, they once again picked up their glasses.

"To you," Donovan said simply.

"To us," Marissa replied.

They kissed and drank and kissed some more. Champagne kisses, in fact, that would eventually lead to a lifetime of bubbly love.

* * * * *

REQUEST YOUR FREE BOOKS!

2 FREE NOVELS
PLUS 2 FREE GIFTS!

KIMANI™
ROMANCE

Love's ultimate destination!

KROM11B

A brand-new miniseries featuring fan-favorite authors!

THE HAMILTONS *Laws of Love*

Family. Justice. Passion.

Ann Christopher	Pamela Yaye	Jacquelin Thomas

Available September 2012	*Available October 2012*	*Available November 2012*

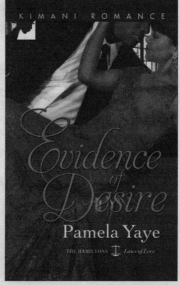

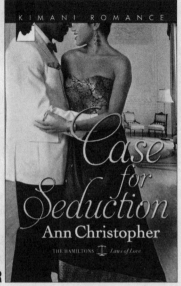

Harlequin® Desire

ALWAYS POWERFUL, PASSIONATE AND PROVOCATIVE.

A BRAND-NEW WESTMORELAND FAMILY NOVEL FROM *NEW YORK TIMES* BESTSELLING AUTHOR

BRENDA JACKSON

Megan Westmoreland needs answers about her family's past. And Rico Claiborne is the man to find them. But when the truth comes out, Rico offers her a shoulder to lean on…and much, much more. Megan has heard that passions burn hotter in Texas. Now she's ready to find out….

TEXAS WILD

"Jackson's characters are…hot enough to burn the pages."
—*RT Book Reviews* on *Westmoreland's Way*

Available October 2 from Harlequin Desire®.

HD73198K